IMPORTANT THINGS
THAT DON'T MATTER

IMPORTANT THINGS THAT DON'T MATTER

DAVID AMSDEN

wm

WILLIAM MORROW

An Imprint of HarperCollins*Publishers*

IMPORTANT THINGS THAT DON'T MATTER. Copyright © 2003 by David Amsden. All rights reserved. Printed in the United States of America. No part of this book may be used or reproduced in any manner whatsoever without written permission except in the case of brief quotations embodied in critical articles and reviews. For information address HarperCollins Publishers Inc., 10 East 53rd Street, New York, NY 10022.

HarperCollins books may be purchased for educational, business, or sales promotional use. For information please write: Special Markets Department, HarperCollins Publishers Inc., 10 East 53rd Street, New York, NY 10022.

FIRST EDITION

Designed by Fearn Cutler de Vicq

Printed on acid-free paper

Library of Congress Cataloging-in-Publication Data

Amsden, David.
Important things that don't matter / David Amsden.—1st ed.
p. cm.
ISBN 0-06-051388-8
1. Children of divorced parents—Fiction. 2. Fathers and sons—Fiction.
3. Boys—Fiction. I. Title.
PS3601.M76 P57 2003
813'.6—dc21   2002068556

03 04 05 06 07 JTC/RRD 10 9 8 7 6 5 4 3 2 1

Mom:

This book is yours

PART ONE

ADULTHOOD

My God, I am young, young, and I didn't even know it; they didn't even tell me, that I was young.

—William Faulkner, *Absalom, Absalom*

UP LATE WITH DAD AND SHIRLEY

Dad will be waiting at the gate.

That was the plan. It was late, well past midnight, like the latest I'd ever known the world with eyes open. Me and Mom were exhausted from the flight, me letting loose these dizzying yawns every twenty seconds as the plane taxied in, the whites of Mom's eyes all stained with bloodshot tributaries. The tendons in my hand still stung from Mom's squeezing it the second the landing gear opened up—she didn't let go until it was clear we were down, clear no one around her was burning to death. Mom hated takeoffs and landings, was convinced we all got only so many. You'd see this in her eyes at times, and not just when planes were involved—this fear-stained look, like something tragic was coming right at her, right there nipping at her earlobes.

I leaned my head on the little oval window, checked out the flat landscape: runways and windsocks, these sparks in the dark, going from two- to three-dimensional, thanks to the pinpoint flashing lights of white, green, blue, red. I looked at the lights until my eyes watered up, the colors blending inside them, forming these wild shapes. Then I'd have to blink and start over. Out in the distance you could see Dulles, all whitewashed and glowing, its roof like a frozen wave begging to crash.

The plane stopped now, completely, fasten-seatbelt signs binged off, the overhead fluorescents flooded the cabin, making everyone's face tough to stomach: all green-yellow, pasty. Their eyes were gray. People getting their bags out from the overheads now, the silence was broken up by the cracking of knees, fingers, shoulders, toes, elbows, necks.

"Sit tight, honey," Mom was saying, getting our things in order, putting my Crayolas back in their box—

"Do you want to hang on to the red?"

"Yes." I had a thing for carrying the red one in my pocket.

—and now my He-Man coloring book, now my die-cast Corvette Stingray and the G.I. Joe sniper expert who was into using the car as a skateboard. All shoved into her purse, next to her how-to-make-your-business-work book, or her how-not-to-stress-out-while-making-your-business-work book, or whatever she was reading, which always had something to do with self-improvement.

I kept busy by smashing my forehead against the plastic window, feeling my nose turn to Play-Doh. I pretty much thought about half the universe in terms of Play-Doh then. In school we'd started playing with it, making Play-Doh alphabets, each of us assigned one letter. Twenty-five of us in the class, my name starting with an A, I got to do A and Z. This made all the kids wish I was dead, but really, I could've cared less about the letters—I just liked eating the stuff, how it got all salty. You know, like ocean-flavored bubble gum.

"Stop that," Mom was saying.

I was now pressing my open mouth against the window, inflating my cheeks. Drawing smiley faces on the plastic with my tongue.

"I want to be home."

"Well, licking that filthy window's not gonna bring home here any quicker," Mom pointed out.

———

Now Mom was saying come on, let's go, said we're ready and took my hand, led me out into the aisle in front of her. Mom kept her hand on my head as we skittered down the aisle, having to stop every second for old people, who all had to look at me with the same glazed empty smile. The stewardesses looked as sleepy as Mom standing in the doorway, their makeup starting to flake off, smeared like someone sent them through a carwash by mistake, waving good-bye, sleep well, bye, bye now, good-bye. To me one went—

"Sleep tight."

—and the other, squatting down, went—

"Don't let the bedbugs bite, you cutie."

—which always freaked me out, that little rhyme. I mean, do you know anyone who has any idea what bedbugs are? And, say you're asleep, how can you make sure they don't bite you? It's funny how when you get older, you realize half of what adults tell you as a kid is meant to turn you into a crazed insomniac by the time you hit twenty. I'm twenty now, so trust me. I know what I'm talking about.

———

The tunnel leading to the gate was even brighter than in the plane, and cold. We'd been in Florida, so this was my first time feeling cold in about a week. At five years old this is a substantial chunk of time. We'd been visiting a friend of Mom's, some lady she knew in high school who was stuck in Florida because her dad was about to die. You know, because old people are always going down to Florida to die. It was all sad, I know, but I didn't really understand. Every time we went to the hospital to visit the dad I'd be stuck in some room with a thousand other kids my age, some day-care center run, as they all are, by a psychotic old lady. Not that I cared—there were enough crayons and construction paper in there that after fifteen minutes I'd have no idea where I was.

"Oh it's cold," I was saying.

"I thought you told winter to go away before we got back," Mom said, taking me by the hand.

"I did."

"Are you sure?"

"I did, I swear."

"Then why's it still cold?"

"I don't know. When are we going to be home?"

"I know, sweetie," she said, all patting my head. "Real soon. I'm tired too."

———

He'd be right there at the gate.

That was the plan. With Mom pretty much everything pivoted around some master plan—she hasn't had the best of luck and I guess it's her way of keeping tragedy at bay. I don't know. I just know that this plan went: Dad would be there, at the gate, so happy to see us, his moustache doing that thing it did when he smiled, where it looked all caught up in some breeze. And he wouldn't be sleepy, not a bit. He worked nights at Jerry's and knew these hours, knew hours ten times later than this. He'd take us to the baggage claim, and he'd carry all our bags. Dad would have the car nearby, that little blue Honda, and before me and Mom knew what was what, we'd be at home, in bed, asleep, at home, finally—

"Shit shit *shit*," Mom was suddenly going.

Out of the tunnel now, we were standing at the gate.

"*Shit,*" she said again.

"Mom?"

"Oh excuse me. Damn it. I'm sorry," she said. She looked around the gate some more. The plane hadn't been too full, and most of the passengers were already on their way to the baggage claim. So the gate was pretty much empty, buzzing with the kinds of lights I can't stand. You know, the kind that are never turned off. They burn out instead.

"Goddamn it. *Damn* it."

"What?" I asked.

"Your father's not here."

"Where is he?"

"I don't know."

"Maybe he's lost."

"Maybe. He was supposed to come with Shirley."

"How come?"

"I don't know. Damn this."

"We'll be home soon?" I wanted to know.

"Oh I'm sorry," Mom said. She closed her eyes, now took a breath, took another, like suddenly she was asthmatic. "Let's get our bags. Maybe your father's down there."

———

Shirley moved into our house that year, 1986. Dad and Mom had been renting out one of the basement rooms since they moved in, for extra cash. The first boarder was an old lady whose family found her one day, apologized to my parents, drove her away, and put her in a nursing home, where she died a week later. Then we had Shirley, the first in my lifetime. I always liked her a lot.

She was twenty-seven, the same age as Dad, just younger than Mom. She had this boy-short brown hair, a pointy nose, these big glazy brown eyes, a jawline like a boomerang, and lips that could mess men up if they looked the wrong way, which they were always doing anyway. There was something else about Shirley that men in 1986 fell apart over: she happened to be an ex-Playmate, had been out in L.A. for years, living at the Mansion, serving up cocktails to whoever in one of those old-school pink bunny getups. I'm not even kidding.

Then she got the splendid news about her mother: that one night out of nowhere she had axed her father to death while he was sleeping, cut his hands and feet off first, clogged the toilet with them, then went after his insides. She lived in some crap apartment, which is how the cops caught her: with the toilet clogged, the downstairs neighbors got flooded, called the super, and you can figure out the rest.

Which is why Shirley was living with us, back in Maryland, back to Rockville, her hometown from years ago. She was settling jail stuff (her mom got life), burial stuff (there was no funeral), and legal stuff. The lady was about to cash in on a small inheritance that would screw up her life forever.

———

Dad wasn't anywhere around the baggage claim either, which is why Mom was again going—

"Goddamn it. Damn this."

"Maybe he's just lost."

"You're right," she said. "Maybe. I'm sorry. I don't know."

The baggage carousel ground on: the angled aluminum

conveyer belt, moving all clumsy, so slow. I wanted to put my foot up on it and see what would happen, put it right up here and—

"*Don't* do that!" Mom snapped.

"But—"

"No."

"But I was just—"

"Honey, I'm at the end of my line here. I'm at the end."

"Okay."

"Where the hell is your father?"

I only had this small Spiderman backpack, used it as a carry-on, so we were just waiting for Mom's suitcase, one of those gigantic kinds with wheels and a leash. It was the last to come out.

"I see it, Mom. Can I get it?"

"Another time," she said, pulling the thing over the moving rubber railing. "Come on. Let's check for him out here."

We went out to where the cabs and buses pull up. The lights everywhere were this dusty yellow glow. You know, the kind that lights up every parking lot in America after a certain hour. There was lots of concrete, a few men directing traffic. It smelled like car exhaust and garbage, was so cold my joints felt freeze-dried. There weren't many people, and those around were disappearing quick, into cabs, into cars, fading out there into the parking lot, this spread of cars all shiny and still under the lights.

God, was it cold, really so cold—

"Mom, I'm *freezing*."

"Me too, me too."

"When are we going to be *home*?"

"I'm cold too," is all Mom said. "I know. I'm cold too."

———

Shirley lived downstairs with her boyfriend, this nine-foot-tall German guy with thin blond hair down to his chin. I liked him too. He drove a gold Porsche 922. You know, the kind that wasn't around for long, the kind that looked like a cheese wedge.

There had been this one time where Shirley and her boyfriend were the only ones with me at the house and a small crisis broke out: Mom and Dad had just bought one of those pop-top campers, the cheap kind that looked like Smurf huts, and Dad had taken Mom's puke-green Volvo to the shop to get a trailer hitch put on. You won't believe what happened. The man at the shop forgot to put the emergency brake in place when he put the car up on the lift. So while he's working, the Volvo ends up rolling backward, right into his face, shatters his neck in two. The guy was dead on the spot.

So there's Dad, stuck with the car on top of a dead mechanic and the cops were saying they needed it for a few hours, to try to make sense of everything. And Dad had to get to Jerry's for the late shift. He called Shirley at the house and before I know what's what, she and her boyfriend are shoving me into the hatchback part of the Porsche since there's no backseat, crammed me in under the curved glass, kept in place by a thousand sofa cushions. You should have seen how fast this guy drove. I could hear the engine back there, really hear it, the ball bearings screaming at each other, how it went from low to high over and over, how it turned dead silent for a split second between gears. I closed my eyes and suddenly we were flying to the moon. We'd hit a pothole and to me we had just grazed an asteroid. Sharp turns and we were circling Saturn's rings. We were off to meet Sally Ride, who I knew was pretty with long curly brown hair. We were off to meet her, and all the other astronauts we wouldn't shut up about in school ever since they blew up in the *Challenger*.

———

Me and Mom were running through the whole airport now. Or at least Mom was walking fast and I had to keep pace by running. It was quick, fragmented, all panicked. The big windows of Dulles jet black with night, the walls and ceiling the whitest thing I'd ever seen. The night cleaners were out with their humming wax machines, and the floor—so bright and smooth you thought you were running around inside an ice cube, everything flashing silver with each step. I was so tired, but had to keep going, had to stay with Mom.

She looked so worried, so scared, her eyes all dry-looking now, more yellow than white. We went back to the gate, back to the baggage claim, down the east wing, the west wing, over and over, everything white or black, these cool crisp lines, the floor blending into ceiling, ceiling into floor, all lit with invisible lights, my shoulder popping in and out of its socket as Mom yanked me in ten thousand directions. Mom was sort of murmuring the whole time, whispering to herself, nothing I could make out too clear. Every now and then we'd pass a couple, or a family, or two friends, some sort of groggy reunion. Looking at these clean people, I felt so embarrassed my teeth hurt.

Mom stopped, stood still for a moment. She said we needed a phone. Mind you, she didn't mean a pay phone—she'd already tried one of them, called home and got only rings. She was now talking about one of those phones you never want to use, the kind found in places like malls and airports that broadcast over the loudspeakers. The kind of phones, basically, used only by people whose lives are messed up. Even when you're five the last thing you want to be in the world is the type of person who relies on these phones.

So I said—

"Mom, maybe he's outside. Maybe he's—"

"We were *just* out there. What do you want from me?"

"What?"

"I'm sorry, I'm sorry," Mom said. "Not you."

Then she said we have to use this phone. Mom said she was at the end of her line. She picked up the receiver, which was bright red. It was the type of phone you picture in a tank or submarine, and even in there it's a last resort. Normally, there was an operator to relay your message, but it was so late right now that the operator was off, and you had to do it yourself. So Mom followed the directions, dialed whatever combination of numbers you had to dial to get on the loudspeaker, and suddenly there was this audible click. You could hear it. She hadn't spoke yet but you could hear we were on. Yes, that's us. We are the ones using this phone. Help us. We are the ones who need it. We are the ones in need. We are the ones going—

"This call is for Joseph Ames. This call is for Joseph Ames. . . ."

It was never cool hearing Mom refer to Dad as Joseph, weird enough when she called him Joe instead of Dad. Kids hate things like this, these reminders that there's so much you don't know.

"Joseph, this is Susan. Your son and I have been looking all over for you. . . ."

I swear it was the only sound in all of Dulles, really so loud, ricocheting off the walls, off the windows. I wished it would just break through the glass and be gone, but all it did was keep colliding with itself instead.

"We went to the gate, Joe, and then to the baggage claim. You weren't there. You weren't. So we went outside, and didn't find you. You weren't outside, Joe, so we went back to the gate—"

She broke off.

"Joe, we are at the emergency phone. In the south corner. If you hear this, please could you come and pick us up?"

When she hung up I asked what are we going to do now. Sit tight, she said, we'd sit tight for a bit, that was about all we could do. If everything went well, he'd be here soon enough. Dad will, and we'll be home.

————

The hour or so we waited by the phone, sitting on the floor right under it, felt like forever, even though I was asleep the whole time, sprawled out with my head on Mom's thigh. Mom was tapping me awake now. My spine felt stiff. I was pretty sure we were the only people in the world who had ever been awake this long and this late.

God, Mom was crying—

"Mom?"

She stood up, took my hand, sort of yanked me to my feet, started walking.

"Mom?"

She picked up the pace, me taking these little skip-steps to keep up.

"Mom?"

"I . . . I don't know—"

"Mom? My back hurts. Mom?"

She kept changing pace, all fast then slow. Our footsteps echoed.

"I know . . . I know, I know, I just don't know. I just don't know what to do. What do I do? Why in the hell does he do this shit—"

"Mom? You're hurting my arm, Mom."

"Oh my God." She stopped. "I'm sorry," she said. "Oh my God. Look, I'm so sorry." She squatted down, looked right into me. Her eyes were so red I couldn't even look at them. I was looking at her forehead instead. "Should we get a cab? What should we do? I'm sorry. Is that what we should do?"

"Mom, I don't know," I said.

"Jesus," she said. "The last thing I want to do is spend thirty dollars on a cab."

———

We were going back downstairs now, back past the baggage claim. All the carousels were off. We went outside again where the cabs pull up. There were none, nothing. It was freezing.

"Where are the cabs?" I wanted to know.

We went up to some guy, a black man in a big puffy blue jacket. He was just standing there, outside, but he didn't look cold at all.

"Do you work here?" Mom asked.

He nodded.

"So you can get a cab for us?"

"Ain't easy at this hour," he said.

"Is it possible?"

"Possible, yes. But pretty much a matter of luck."

"I don't understand. What are you saying? What are we supposed to do?"

"As I said, pretty much a matter of luck." I swear the guy was practically laughing.

"Jesus Christ. Do you work here?"

He nodded again.

"You work here, for chrissake. Isn't it your job to get us a goddamn cab?"

"At this hour, it's—"

"God*damn* it. *Damn* it. You *work* here and it's your goddamn *job* to get me a taxi and—"

"Ain't no flights coming in for hours, cabbies know this."

"I don't understand," Mom said. "Pardon me, but I just

don't get it. I just don't get it. You're out here to get people cabs. My son and I need a cab. And now—"

"Look, ma'am—"

"And now, goddamn it, now you tell me it's *luck*? My little boy's freezing here. Look at him. . . . *Look* at him. He's cold and tired and my husband was supposed to—"

"*Ma'am.*"

"My God," she said. I grabbed her leg. "God, I'm sorry. I'm sorry. Look, I'm sorry. But what the hell am I supposed to do? Just tell me that, please. We were supposed to be picked up by my . . . What the hell do we do?"

It was almost funny how unconcerned this guy came off, like he had this same conversation every night with two people who looked exactly like me and Mom. I turned to Mom. You should have seen the way she looked. Her face was all about to fall apart completely now. I mean, her mouth was shaking, cheeks and nose red, all poisoned-looking. I swear, like she was about to split straight down the middle. You could really imagine it: her eyes going dead, then falling off to the sides, then her nose, now that little crease above her lip, split straight in half, her mouth too—

"What in the hell are we supposed to *do*?"

—like she wanted to hit him, *that* was her look. She wanted to take this man, throw him on the pavement, and just start hitting him until some kind of order set in. He knew where Dad was, knew something, and she would beat it out of him. I was so scared now. There's nothing worse than seeing your parents all lit up by emotions that don't mean a thing to you. It's like they don't belong to you anymore, and right there it hits you, slams right up against you really, how unprepared you are for doing anything without them. I just wanted to do something, anything. I'd help her beat the guy if that would help. Mom, I'll do it. I'll go for the shins. I could do that, get him in the shins, and he'd be too slow to catch me. Girls in class had got me in the shins before, so I knew it killed. Something, that would be something. I'll do it, I will, I'll do anything—

Suddenly a car horn starts blaring, echoing, flying right at us off the concrete columns. Everyone looked. Mom, the black guy, me. These two headlights, far off, indistinguishable other than that. Then they come a little closer, and it's clear it's Dad's little blue Honda. You could see him right there in the driver's seat. You could see his moustache even. You could see Shirley too, right there next to him in the passenger's seat.

———

"How ya doin', feller?" Dad was now asking.

I was sitting in the back, next to Shirley. There were candy wrappers all over the floor, always was in that Honda, Caramel Creams mostly. I knew I was supposed to hate Shirley, but I couldn't help how good it felt to be next to her. She smoked a hundred packs of cigarettes a day and still managed to smell only of perfume and clean clothes and Pantene. It was good seeing Dad too, even though it was obvious I was supposed to hate him even more.

"Tired," I said.

Mom got in the passenger's seat now, shut the door, slammed it I guess. Dad lit a cigarette, a Vantage. I leaned on Shirley, closed my eyes, sort of hearing Dad saying—

"Sorry we're a touch late, what happened is—"

But then all you were hearing was Mom shutting him up with—

"I don't even want to hear it, Joe. I couldn't care less."

———

Dad and Shirley were together a lot then. It's funny. Three years later I'd start to get it, the way I'm still getting everything, in fragments, backward, so bear with me. Shirley had moved out by then, I don't know where. Anyway, I come home from school one day, piss off Mom accidentally, and like that she's going off—

". . . that your father does *cocaine* . . . ," she's saying, ". . . do you even know what that *means*?"

And then, one day, years after that, I'm driving around with Dad in his brown VW bus. Maybe I'm thirteen years old now and he's going off about Shirley, how she got this twenty-five-grand inheritance, blew it all on cocaine. All of it gone in one weekend. And he was there. Dad tells me how crazy Shirley was. And since Dad never has any idea when to shut up, he tells me about her body all of a sudden, how beautiful it was. He even tells me how beautiful her breasts were. Especially that one time when she got up on the table, that time she danced for everyone.

PRISON

Floyd's apartment smelled terrible. Like spoiled eggs, smoked-out window curtains, freezer-burned TV dinners, and the singed plastic stench of electrical wiring going to hell. Floyd moved around in this menacing hobble, a daddy longlegs missing half his limbs. The guy was this constant convulsion of tics: the fingers in his right hand jetting straight out, then clenching up; his left eye drooping down slow, then whipping back into place; always making these sniffing sounds with his nose, like a dog looking for a place to piss. He was so skinny that I was scared to ever see him with his shirt off, was convinced he was only organs and bones. And with Floyd you always ran the risk of seeing him naked. He only wore this one bathrobe, terry cloth, paisley patterned, pine green and dark purple. It was the kind of thing a circus freak-show regular sports around the dressing room.

But Floyd was no bearded lady. He was this guy that Dad had started hanging out with lately, like all the time. And right now he was all up in my face like—

"Jesus Christ, Joe! You gotta li'l boy for *real*! Well, Jesus. This is your li'l boy!"

His breath was all cigarette smoke. His gums were bright red in parts, glassy-looking. The other parts were almost black.

"I know, I know," Dad said.

"A li'l boy! Look at 'm! Looks just like you! Spi't an' image!"

"How are things?" Dad said.

"Same as ever," Floyd said. "How old is this guy? How old are you?"

"Six," I said. "Six and a quarter. Going on seven."

"Oh when I was sixteen," Floyd said, "my golly! You shoulda *seen* it, wild as hell! Great time! Hot damn! Joe, you know what I'm talkin' about, doncha Joe?"

"Work goin' all right?" Dad asked.

"Too much goddamn work," Floyd said. "Other than that, fine as feathers." Floyd peered down at me again. His eye was doing its thing. He had about three strands of red hair left on his head—the rest was a yellowy gray, and frizzy. And he had freckles all over his face just like Tyler, the orange-haired kid in my class who everyone was scared of. You know, the types who look like the descendants of red ants. "So you been with Dad tonight, huh?" Floyd said. "Whatchu guys been up to?"

"We went to the movies," I said.

"Oh yeah? Which one?"

"*Muppets Take Manhattan.*"

"*Muppets Take Manhattan*, huh? Okay, okay. Seen the previews. Li'l puppet guys. Hermit the frog! Kids still into Hermit the Frog? Jesus! Things don't change, do they Joe?"

Dad smiled. Floyd kept talking.

"So whadya think? Good movie?"

"I like New York," I said. "So it was awesome."

"Whadya think, Joe? This kid know what he's talkin' about?"

"Sure does."

"Jesus, he really looks just like you, Joe," Floyd said. "Don't he?"

"Dad, you were asleep the whole time," I said. One thing about Dad, he was sort of always asleep the whole time, especially during something like a Muppet movie.

"Oh I was just restin' my eyes, feller. When you get to be my age," Dad said, "you can see right through the lids."

"Can not."

"Can too," Dad said. "Floyd, am I lyin'?"

"Straight through 'em!" Floyd said. "Straight through the damn things."

———

Three things happened in 1987: Desi died, Opa died, Mom and Dad split up. Desi's dying made everything else seem like pretty much nothing. Desi had been my first dog, this black-and-white sheltie, and when Mom sat me down on the living room couch's knobby white cushions and told me what happened, I lost it.

Desi, she explained, had met another dog during his morning walk, some mammoth German shepherd. They got to playing, so rough Mom and the other dog's owner had to let go of the leashes—they were getting all tangled up. The dogs then ran out into the middle of Nelson Street, right in front of the house. They were playing right at the top of the hill, you know, and because they were there, well, the car couldn't see them. Do you understand? Do you know what that means? The car couldn't see them, couldn't hit the brakes in time. And now Desi was dead. My face felt all blistered up, I was crying so hard.

So maybe I was used to things when she sat me down in

the exact same place a few weeks later and told me about Opa, my grandfather on her side, her dad. Opa had been in and out of the hospital for months. I knew all of Mom's family was going crazy over it, but it never really bothered me. I mean, old people are hard for really young people to love—even when you're related to them, they're frightening. And Opa was especially terrifying because he was bald, big, smart as hell, and Polish, went through the Holocaust and all that. He couldn't say anything without yelling at the top of his lungs, always using words I didn't understand, let alone saying them in this gravelly accent that happened to be identical to every bad guy in every cartoon I loved. You know what Opa was? He was Gargamel without the cat.

It wouldn't be until later, until now really—when all anyone does is tell me how much I'm like Opa, the way people can never tell if I like them or not, or if I meant to be funny—that I started missing the guy. It's simple: anytime anyone tells you about someone who would have loved you, and who you would have loved back, you can't help but feel incriminated. You feel like everyone's blaming you.

Anyway, a few weeks after that, here's Mom again: sitting me down again in the same place, the pattern of the cushions etched into my ass at this point, saying—

"I have something to tell you."

"Okay," I said.

"Your father isn't going to be living here anymore."

"How come?"

"Well," she said, "with Jerry's gone, he's going to be very busy, and, well . . . and he's going to be moving out."

I realize I forgot to tell you about Jerry's. I'm sorry. I'm remembering things here, and they don't come in the right order.

So here you go: Jerry's was this pizza place where Dad worked, some kind of local chain, plastic tabletops meant to look like wood, curvy red plastic seats, all that. I think Dad was the manager. All he did was go in late, sit in this office with fake wood walls, and count money. He counted it, put it in these thick plastic envelopes, with thick zippers and padlocks. He lost the job when the store closed down. I think it closed because he didn't really count the money right, put most of it up his nose, but I've never bothered asking. To me Jerry's was, and will always be, about two things: spray bottle wars with this black kid Shareef, who worked there, and unlimited free french fries. I was five years old, so you tell me what else really matters.

"Okay," I was saying to Mom.

"But he'll still visit," Mom was saying, "and you'll see him all the time."

"Okay."

"Honey," Mom said. Her face was shaking, by the way. "Honey, your father and I are getting a divorce."

"Oh."

"Do you know what divorce is?"

"It means Dad won't live here anymore, but I'll still see him."

This statement really seemed to get to Mom. Parents hate it when they don't need to explain anything to their kids—they don't know what to do with themselves anymore.

"That's it exactly," she finally said. She was almost impossible to make out, the way she was whispering like that. "Exactly."

"Okay," I said. "When are we getting a new dog?"

———

How did someone like Mom, a Jewish woman with European parents, real educated types, American citizens because of the Holocaust, both professors, end up married to someone like Dad, a pale Catholic kid from a farm up in middle-of-nowhere Maine? It's funny. That's what everyone always wants to know, and what I never really think about. But so you know, they met at this ice-cream parlor, sometime around 1975. Mom was just out of college and starting her graphic design company, the same little firm she has today, and asked could she design the menus, draw up the logo. Dad was behind the counter, because his brother Ray owned the shop, had moved down from Maine to start it up, and Dad moved down with him because working there was a lot better than lifting potatoes and whatever else he had to do on the farm. The story goes Mom liked watching Dad's arms when he scooped the ice cream, which I'll admit have always been great-looking, still are, permanently cut from doing farm work as a kid. So she liked looking at them, liked watching the muscles tighten up, stretching out the T-shirt sleeves, and before anyone knows what's going on she's not only designed the menu and drawn up the logo, she's married Dad too, had a little boy with him. I guess it's an interesting story, but as you can see, before I knew what was what they were divorced, so I've never really cared.

The worst thing about the divorce, really, was Floyd. Dad got me three days a week and in the beginning Floyd was around for at least two of them. Dad was living with Uncle Ray, his brother, who at this point had given up the ice-cream shop, got a degree, and landed some kind of well-paying business job—I don't know what it was, just that Ray was always getting richer. This was all when Ray was still married, lived with Aunt Edie in some townhouse near what was now Mom's house in Rockville. Dad had this cool waterbed mattress in the basement, where the walls were wood beams and that bright Pink Panther insulation, the floor concrete so cold you were always in socks. It was a good setup, because I liked hanging out with Ray's kids.

There was Cousin Mike, who was a year younger than me, weaker than me, and therefore fun to play with. And there was Cousin Stacey, who was three years older than me and had a best friend who one time, as a joke, took her underwear off and sat down on my face until my nose disappeared.

But Dad was always saying we couldn't hang around the house, said it was rude to his brother. It was just a temporary thing, until everything worked itself out. It's funny how after divorces, temporary things seem to become permanent elements of adults' lives. Or at least that was always the case with Dad.

So we always had to find something to do. Movies were popular. *Top Gun. Adventures in Baby-sitting. Death Wish IV.* Anything with Chuck Norris. So were bars, especially this one I'll tell you about in a second, which inevitably led to us visiting a church, something I've always hated. Or Breakers Billiards, the pool hall in downtown Rockville lit only with black lights, like making sure you could never figure out what time it was when you were in there. And Floyd. Who the hell was Floyd? We would go to Floyd's house all the time. Dad knew I hated it there, hated how I smelled afterward. But he always said it would put hair on my chest, and I had nothing on that.

———

Floyd was in the kitchen now. I never liked sitting on his sofa because, with the plastic still on the cushions, the thing pinched and squeaked, like sitting on a ferret or something. So I tossed aside a gun magazine, sank down into the La-Z-Boy. God, it reeked of Floyd, but so did everything else and eventually you got used to it. Then you left and it was all over you.

Floyd came out of the kitchen now with a Coke for me, two cans of beer for him and Dad. The fridge, he explained, was busted. Did we mind drinking them at room temperature?

"Well, okay then!" Floyd was saying. "Here's to the . . . to the . . . to the Muppets!"

"To the Muppets," Dad said.

"Hermit the Frog!" Floyd said.

"It's Kermit," I said.

"What's that?"

"Kermit."

"Well, speakin' a frogs . . . ," Floyd said, "how's about we watch another movie? A little cinematic wonderment? Wanna watch another movie?"

"Okay," I said.

"Lemme findja somethin'." He crawled down on his hands and knees, going all through the movies he had stuffed under the VCR. It's not like I wanted to notice, but I couldn't help see that his robe had drifted up, showing off these fiery swirls of hair on his pink thighs. You know those

rip each other to
ın? The ones where
that was looking at
s does he like, Joe?

ıg and slid it in the

ɔyd are just gonna be
ıy? We'll be right in
ng, okay?"

ɔyd was saying. "He

ɛ way, started up in the
obviously a jail. A cop

ıcting up?" the cop was

ʌıu the guard. "But they're
a feisty bunch."

"Feisty? That so?" They both talked funny, all exaggerated but slow, like the words were difficult to pronounce. The cop was scratching his chin, but not like he was thinking hard. "What's the warden say?"

"The warden doesn't know."

"Well, between you and me, the warden don't *need* to know."

"I'm not sure I'm understanding."

"Heh heh. Oh, give it time, Charlie," the cop said. "Give it some time. You just let me have a word with one of the inmates. Who's the leader?"

The next scene was an interrogation room, a steel table, two chairs, gray cinderblock walls, very brightly lit. The cop was sitting by himself, cigarette in his mouth. There was a knock on the door.

"Come in," the cop said.

I was surprised to see what the leader looked like. In every other action movie I'd seen, this was always some foreign guy, Russian or Mexican, with cratered skin, and some campy accessory like a python around his neck, a white rat with a leash attached to some diamond encrusted collar, brass knuckles made out of some rare crystal. But this leader, for one thing, was a woman, and very American-looking at that. She was tall, with long blond hair that didn't even move when she walked, dark eyebrows so perfect they looked like two thin strips of hot tar.

"What the hell are you doing here?" she asked.

"Looks like I just can't leave you alone," he said.

"What are we going to do about it then?"

"My temper's thinning with you lady," he said.

"Oh is it now?" she said.

What's funny is he didn't seem so angry, was still all stunted and awkward, but suddenly, like someone hit a switch, the guy's standing up, pounding his hands on the table. He kicked the chair into the wall. "Get over here!" he yelled, but he gave her no time, was already moving over to her. "Come here, you bitch!" he yelled. He grabbed her by the collar of her orange prison garb. "You fucking bitch!" he yelled again. "Do you realize what you've put me through?"

"Oh you know you like it," she said.

"Shut up lady."

He unzipped the front of her jumpsuit, a zipper that went all the way down to her waist. She wasn't wearing a bra. Being six, the only woman's breasts I'd ever seen were Mom's, and they looked nothing like these. And I don't just mean because Mom didn't have that scorpion tattoo circling her nipple.

"I know what you want," she said.

"You bitch!" the guy said, slamming his face into her breasts. They hardly moved. Then he was back up with his mouth right up against hers, their tongues spinning like colliding helicopter blades. Her lips looked like the wax candy I got every Halloween. You know, the kind given out by the neighborhood freaks who were somehow unaware of the fact that no one liked that stuff. No one ever knew what to do with it.

"Yeah," she was saying. "Call me a bitch. I'm your bitch."

"Fuck you," he said. He slapped her face now, twice. "You whore bitch!"

"Oh yeah," she said. "I like that. Do that again baby. Do that again."

"Shut up," he said, slapping her again.

He pushed her away, into the faraway wall, stepped back but still looking at her all hard. She was taking off her boots, then sliding the rest of her uniform down. She looked at him the whole time, like all angry, the same look girls in class gave you when you stole their *My Little Pony* barrettes. She wore bright red underwear, with a dragon stitched on the front. The back was too thin for anything.

"I know what you want," she said. "I know what all you cops want."

He was naked now. He had also been taking his clothes off. His pants were tight, gave him some trouble. The guy had to hop on one foot, but his face didn't change. This man was dead serious.

"You whore bitch slut!" he called her, smashing himself

against her. He ripped her underwear right off, *Incredible Hulk* style. "You have no idea what I'm about to do to you."

She put her leg on the chair now—somehow it was right there again—and the two of them started shaking, convulsing. They sounded pretty much exactly like joggers. It was this spastic movement, him grabbing a fistful of her hair, saying she wasn't just nothing, but *less* than nothing, nothing but a jailbird, a little whore bitch jailbird slut. But he was wasting his time telling her these things, because all she ever said was that she knew, knew exactly who she was. Her words came out all shaky. She sounded like she was on a roller coaster.

"Don't you stop," she was now saying.

He sort of grunted.

"Don't you dare stop you bastard."

And now he was telling her he wouldn't ever stop. "Beg bitch and I won't even hear," is how he put it. They were both shiny now. She deserved punishment, he said. More punishment than she even knew. "You have no clue," he was saying. "You don't have a clue."

He backed away—I sure didn't *ever* look like *that*. She moved over to the table, supporting herself on her elbows. "Look at that," he said, in a way that you knew he was about to come up with one of his wordy descriptions of her. "Look at that, just like a poodle. Scared as a puppy. Just a little puppy poodle jailbird slut."

He came up behind her. The camera zoomed up into his face. God, he looked so serious, just like the guys on the news. This guy was Dan Rather on the bench press. When the camera zoomed out he was slapping her butt, leaving a patch of red. "And I'm just getting started," he said. "So much punishment you don't even know."

"Yeah," she said. "Just like that. Just like that."

Mom had done this to me before, given me a spanking. It's funny though: I never wanted her to keep doing it. She only did it a few times, only when I really acted up, which I guess I was sort of always doing. It always came in the kitchen, the announcement, the fear, the smack, then me running right into my bedroom, propelled by the pain, scorched tears all out of my eyes, down my cheeks, burning my skin like they were some kind of acid. Only one time did Dad spank me and it was about the funniest thing. He apologized right afterward, came into my bedroom and wouldn't shut up about how sorry he was. I was pretty used to it by then, so I had already stopped crying, but now he was the one crying, saying he's sorry, so sorry, please, please forgive me feller, all that. I sat on the bottom bunk of my bed, telling him not to worry. I was the one who had to tell Dad that everything would be okay.

———

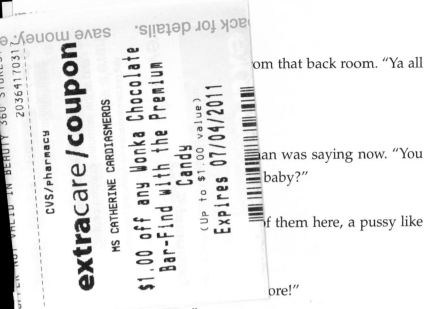

om that back room. "Ya all

an was saying now. "You baby?"

f them here, a pussy like

ore!"

just give us a sec."

"I'll kill you if you don't shut up," the cop was saying. "I swear to God I'll kill you."

———

When Dad and Floyd finally came out, sneezing and sniffing like they went off and caught colds, the entire cast of the film was in the mess hall. They were all naked, about ten men, ten women. The men were all calling the women bitches and whores and the women were telling the men how much they liked it. I think Floyd laughed, made some comment about the merits of independent film, show-offy, and got no response out of me or Dad. Sometimes the camera would cut to a slow motion shot, a crippled-looking man's face, a woman looking bored to death. In the middle of it all was this old man, looked about seventy, with these bushy white eyebrows igniting right out of his forehead. He was wearing those big thick sunglasses that blind men and retired people wear. He was also a midget. I've always been good at finding the subtle things in movies, and figured he was the warden—they had kept talking about how he was small, how he couldn't really see. The plan had been for the women to break out. They were conspiring with the guards and the cops, that was the movie's point, but things like this kept happening. It was frustrating to watch. These people had no focus. You bitch ass whore slut. Yeah, that's what I am, that's exactly what I am. And you're my daddy, that's what you are. Shut up. Shut up. My daddy, you know you are, you're my daddy—

But what's so funny, what I really want to tell you about, is that a few years later, in middle school, this kid Dan invites me to sleep over at his house. His parents go off to bed, and he goes into some closet, fishes out a movie. And I'm not even kidding when I tell you it was the same goddamn tape. So the movie's playing, but I'm not really paying attention. I'm just hearing Dad coming up to me that day at Floyd's, practically feeling his moustache brushing up against my ear, hearing him saying it's time to go. He's asking me to please not tell Mom about the movie, and right there at Dan's it hits me that she still didn't know about that day. And then I realized that maybe Dan was gay or something, because all he ever told me was how strong I looked, and with the movie on now all he kept talking about was how you could see the microphone dangling at the top of the screen, like it was some big, hysterical deal. He was obsessed, couldn't be quiet about it. He was laughing so hard he wasn't even making sounds. Look at that! Look at that! It's so cheap! It's so cheap it's funny!

SATURDAY AFTERNOON
COMEDY HOUR

I liked the place because it had one of these glossed-up bars lined with padded chipped-vinyl piping, the kind of place you're likely to come across today only at a Howard Johnson's motel in the middle of some place you'd rather not be. Not that I liked the bar for any reasons related to sentimentality, irony, or kitsch. I was seven years old, skinny, short for my age. So I could rest my chin up on it, hook it right there, stare at my own reflection in the petrified sheen, let my whole body go slack and not worry for a second about falling.

"Getchu another Coke?" the bartender was asking me.

I looked up at Dad. He sort of half looked at me and shrugged, looked real tired. I guess he was always half looking at you all sleepy and shrugging, when I really think about it—either that or he was excited as hell. He was smoking a Vantage. His hair, jet black streaked with white, was greasy as always, like someone was slipping cooking oil into his shampoo bottle when he left the house.

I told the bartender yes, another Coke please.

This was one of my favorite aspects of Saturday afternoons with Dad: Anywhere we went, which pretty much was only this place, I could drink as much Coke as I wanted. I can't remember the bar's name, only that it was in some part of Rockville that's now a fancy mall. The bartenders all knew me, served me in the pint glasses, more for the money. I used two straws, sucked until my cheeks went numb, downing one after another. That's how it was: Dad right there, and me getting all sorts of jittery and so wide awake my eyes felt like someone had torn the lids right off.

"Wanna race?" I asked Dad.

We played this game that I could never get enough of, and was lucky in that Dad was equally obsessed. With Dad a lot of things ended up being turned into games—it's one of his best qualities, from a seven-year-old's perspective anyway. The rules were simple: we each got two straws, me the long white ones, Dad the teeny kind the olives came on.

Count to three, and then we'd both suck hard as we could, seeing who'd finish his drink first.

"If you don't mind losing," Dad said.

"You mean if *you* don't mind losing," I said back, wishing I could've come up with something a little better.

"Whatever ya say, partner," he said, taking the olives off the straw. "Hey," Dad said to the bartender, "gotta sec?"

I want to tell you that the bartender was this hulking, jocular guy, with chapped lips, a squinty mouth, reddish cheeks—a clean shaven Santa Claus for all practical purposes. But because of my chin-on-the-bar frame, I'd be lying if I said I remember more than a disembodied head and a hearty paunch, always in a starched-and-stained white button-down. And an apron—he always had on a white apron. He knew the game well. That's why right now he was saying—

"I see we've gotta rematch. Who won the last one again?"

"I did."

"Barely," Dad said. "Only 'cause I letcha."

"Did not."

"Okay, okay. Enough you two," the bartender said. "Let's try to act like professionals here."

"He started it," Dad said.

"Hey, do you remember that time two seconds ago when I said 'enough'?" the bartender said. "When we were gonna be a couple of pros here? Okay then. You two ready?"

I had switched positions, was now kneeling up on the stool. This was always risky because back then all I ever wore was sweatpants, which slid around like crazy because the stools were vinyl, they swiveled too, and I only weighed slightly more than a true anorexic. But like I said, I was short for my age so this was the only way I could get the right angle. And look, I'd been serious about winning the game, and I may have won the last one, that's true, but it's not like Dad was some rookie.

"Take your marks," the bartender was now saying.

Me and Dad put the straws in our mouths. I could feel him looking at me through the corner of his eye, trying to throw me off. You know, making some stupid face I'd laugh at anyway. But I wasn't looking. I wasn't about to give him the satisfaction.

The bartender was counting down—

"... and ... two ... and ... *three!* Let's see it!"

Through the corner of my eye I monitored Dad's triangular glass, watched the clear liquid get lower and lower, this inverted pyramid being sucked into its own apex. He had less to drink than I did, no ice to worry about. I always argued this was unfair. But all he ever told me was that there was literally gasoline in that glass, and if he drank it too fast, he'd go blind.

But right now he was going faster than usual, like really working it—his whole drink gone in two sips before I even crossed the halfway mark. My cheeks hurt from sucking so hard, they felt sour. I tried to ignore the fact that he'd just won by continuing to go at my Coke. You know, like the match was still in heated progress.

But then I heard Dad and his yelling—

"Ah-ha! Gotcha, feller!"

"I believe we have a new champ," the bartender was saying.

"Ah-*ha!*"

Dad's a pale guy, like that farm he's from is in some hick part of Maine where normal levels of pigment are against the law. I swear, he uses SPF 2000 on a cloudy day and still gets a sunburn. But right now it didn't look like the sun had got him, but something else.

He just looked so awake, all of a sudden, and his entire face—nose, cheeks, chin, forehead—was exploding in these raw flashes, bright red, same with the whites of his eyes. His moustache was dripping. And his mouth was all wet-looking, like a baby's. You know, the way a baby's face gets when it's eating. Red and all wet-looking and somewhere right between miserable and excited.

That's Dad right now after winning. The guy didn't look tired at all. He was still yelling—

"Yee-hee!"

"Stop it," I said.

"Whoo-wee!"

—like some sort of lunatic Indian. He looked at me, saw my face all sandblasted with sadness, pissed off at losing. It didn't seem to bother him at all.

"Oh there's always the rematch, feller," he said. "Besides, seven's my lucky number. That was my seventh martini. How many Cokes've you had?"

"I don't know. Thirty maybe."

"See there, makes sense then," he said. "Ya follow? You're seven years old and the last time you beat me it was probably your seventh Coke. See?"

Dad's always been a genius at finding this kind of logic. At seven, it was too confusing for me to bother disagreeing with. I mean, can you figure it out now?

So I just looked at him. He was still kind of laughing and crying. It didn't feel like he was right next to me anymore, if that makes any sense. I just wondered about that wetness all over his face. And then, because I was mad at him for winning, I wondered what would happen if I took a bunch of cocktail napkins, tied them together, and stuffed them in his mouth. You know, like a fuse. And if I lit it—that's what I really wanted to know. I didn't care about him going blind. If I lit it, would Dad catch on fire and blow up and stop laughing like that?

———

With Jerry's gone, Dad worked two jobs now, at Yummy Yogurt and Super Sandwich. Both were in the food court at

Montgomery Mall. This was way before the mall turned all yuppie with fake gold and marble and orange-skinned people who walked around like melting wax sculptures convinced the fake furniture at Crate & Barrel was classy stuff. That's when the old food court was gutted out, stripped raw, then replaced, strangely, with all the same places as before. Except this time around all the places had different names, foreign sounding, adhering to the great American law that if you want to seem real smart and sophisticated, just start using foreign expressions that no one really understands.

But this, Dad's working there, was before Yummy Yogurt became something ridiculous like Café Crème. The mall was not yet packed with stores selling thousand-dollar candles that stank like two-dollar Glade air freshener. Super Sandwich, I think, became Bologna Bistroteque. Then it went out of business.

He didn't work in the back anymore, Dad had no office. He said this was more freeing, gave him room to breathe. "A man needs his space," he said more than a few times— but his space was always right there in front of the cash register. A guy in a toll booth has sweeter accommodations, and doesn't have to bother with the uniforms Dad had to wear: purple-and-white stripes at Yummy Yogurt, that canary-yellow chef's hat at Super Sandwich. Not that any of this bothered me much. See, I was still young enough that a parent working in fast food was this spectacular phenomenon, like something to brag about at recess. Besides, there was this tunnel in the back, connecting all the food court restaurants. I was into skateboarding then, and could bring my board back there, just like Tony Hawk. That's what I'd do while waiting for Dad to get off, which was pretty much all I did when I hung out with Dad, wait for him to get off. But it was great. I'm not even kidding. I'd skate through that metal tunnel, over the smooth concrete floor. McDonald's. Roy Rogers. Saigon Surprise. Bagelrama. Boardwalk Fries. You'd catch slivers of conversations, people complaining about their bosses, about the spoiled kids they serve, about ketchup refills. All of it kind of zipping past me, flashing bright, shooting by, smelling like shit.

———

You should have seen this guy at the end of the bar, how pissed off he was right now.

"Look at 'm!" he was yelling. "A goddamn *sellout!*" He was talking about the man on the television screen. He was old-looking, with a guitar and one of those devices that suspend a harmonica in front of your mouth. "Sold out when he went electric! Goddamn no-good sellout!"

"Cool it, will you?" the bartender said.

"For Pete's sake! Bob Dylan looks like Vincent Price," the man said. "Look at that! Eur-goddamn-*reka!* Bob Dylan's Vincent Price! With an electric guitar!"

A commercial came on and the guy went back to his drink. I was still looking at his face. Around his eyes you could see these thin veins, this purplish webbing. You didn't want to stare at the guy for all that long.

There would never be many people in the bar at this hour, two or three maybe. It all depended on the day and, like pretty much every bar that's open before five o'clock, whatever was going down in a million other people's lives who either took things too seriously or not seriously enough.

And you never knew exactly what time it was in that bar. Some light came in through a small window in the doorway, but this was the only window in the whole place and it was stained glass, red, yellow, and blue, a distorted image of a fat lady with a pint glass in her hand. I think she was dancing. The red glass had absorbed so much sun that it was faded, sort of bleached. So the light coming in was thin, always covered in dust, which was always moving, like cells in a microscope. Like it was alive. The light may have been coming from the sun, but here's the thing: If you insisted it was moonlight, no one in this place would have called you crazy.

"What's in a martini?" I was asking Dad.

"Ah feller," he said. Then he didn't say anything for a while. Sometimes Dad would do that, just forget he was talking to you in the middle of a sentence. But I was a patient kid and didn't care. "Great drink," he finally said. "Vodka and vermouth. Just the tiniest bit of vermouth."

I've never been good at holding grudges. What I mean is, he was still so happy-looking, but now I liked him for it.

"What's vermouth?"

"Pretty much nothin'," Dad said. "A little somethin' for flavor."

"Like maple syrup?"

"Exactly," he said. "Like with pancakes."

"Goddamn Vincent fucking Price!" the man down the bar was saying to the ice in his cup.

"It looks just like water," I said.

"That's the point. Water in a fancy cup," Dad said. "Wanna give her a sip?"

"Bobby Dylan, you no shits good-for-nothing sellout!"

"I don't know," I said.

"Well, it's here when you decide."

"Who's Bob Dylan?" I asked.

"Shut up over there, will you?" the bartender was saying.

"A famous singer," Dad said. "From when your mother was a kid."

———

The bartender was now coming over with his silver canister. I loved watching this. Looking from down low, it all seemed sort of monumental. All these big hands and bodies. The bartender had hairy fingers—I remember that now. These deep voices. The liquid so clear. And the way it filled the triangular glass, right up the sides, like an hourglass being used in space. Just up to the top, about to spill. But somehow it never did.

I had gone back to my Coke for a while, but watching Dad's ninth martini being poured I was reminded of my interest in the drink, so I asked—

"What's it taste like?"

"What's that feller?"

"That martini."

"You mean this martini right here?"

"Your martini," I said.

"Depends on who you ask."

"Can I try?"

"Gimme a second." He took a sip. He took another. Then he zoned out for a minute. "Just testin' her out," he now explained. "Okay feller, go for it."

I didn't get much, but I understood the importance of what was in there. So as Dad slid it down to me, the cocktail napkin damp and shredding, I shifted on the stool. This way I was sitting on my legs again, getting those traction-less extra inches. I could come down on it now from above and just sip the littlest bit. That was the idea.

But, God, it really was like gasoline, that smell—

"Go for it," Dad was saying. "Won't bitecha."

"I don't know."

"Come on! It'll put some hair on your chest."

"But you don't have any hair on your chest."

"Not for lack of tryin'."

"Okay, okay," I said.

I leaned in now.

Oh, but that taste—

How it bit down all over the insides of your mouth, scraped the lining of your throat, singed holes in your stomach. I felt my eyes watering up now, and even the tears hurt—this stuff had already got to my *tears*. I knew the answer now: yes, Dad would have blown right up.

————

"Hang on to the ball there," Dad was saying to me. "Don't lose the ball."

"Fucking no-good-for-nothing Bobby Dylan!"

"Shut up already, will you?"

"Serious stuff martinis, huh feller? It'll pass, just hang on."

"Ah, fuck you!"

"Get the hell out of here. You're through!"

"Fuck you, you hear me? Fucking Vincent Price piece of nothing."

"See there," Dad said. "Not so bad."

"You've got two minutes. Hear me? Two minutes to shut up or get the hell out of here."

"It just takes a second, partner. Then you'll want another sip."

"Fuck you!"

"Take a deep breath," Dad said. "Yeah, there ya go. That a boy. Yeah, yeah."

I was wondering why was Dad talking so funny the whole time, ever since I took the sip. Even in my near-death state, I could hear that his voice was all distorted. Now that the feeling of being ripped apart was passing, I saw what it was: Dad was laughing, he'd been laughing the whole time, really losing it. From the second I took the sip, and still going right now.

I looked over at him. You should have seen it.

I mean, look at the guy: his face on fire, eyes in their sockets like hot coal about to explode. He was laughing so hard, like all over me, not even making sounds, which is why the first thing out of my mouth was—

"It's *not* funny."

"Oh it is!" he said. "You'll see how funny it is!"

He was going crazy, quaking, all bucking on his stool, falling over, grabbing the vinyl piping so hard the drinks down the whole bar shook like they were possessed.

"Bobby fucking Price!"

And this guy hadn't left yet.

"Will you shut up already? Will you?"

This wasn't the bartender talking. It was Dad. He was still laughing, still all scathed-looking.

"This got nothin' to do with you," the man said to Dad.

"Damn it doesn't," Dad said. "Wanna know somethin'?"

"Goddamn *sellout*!" The guy had turned back to the screen, but Dad was still looking at him. And laughing still.

"Hey . . . hey, I'll tell you somethin'," he said, sounding all anxious. Then suddenly his hand was grabbing my shoulder, practically shaking me to death. "See this boy? You see this boy? Do you *see* this boy? This boy's gotta mother. This boy's gotta mother who used to be my wife."

"Dad?"

He was laughing so hard I don't think he even heard me. And I just wanted him to ease up his grip.

"She was my wife, but not anymore. His mother was. She was my wife. That's all," Dad said. "And I'm just sayin' that I'd still love her if she'd let me. That's it—"

"Dad, you're *hurting* me—"

But suddenly he wasn't gripping me anymore, not at all. And when I looked up at him, he was actually gone. It took me about one second to find him and when I did he couldn't even speak anymore he was laughing so hard.

He was on the floor.

He was making that wheezing sound that people make when something is so funny it starts destroying their insides.

And then, it was the strangest thing. Like that he just stopped laughing. There he was, on the linoleum floor, on his back, legs bent. Like he was on a doctor's table or something. His face was going back to normal, but unevenly, some parts bright red now, others so white they almost looked blue. His eyes got really big, like coated in some kind of thick oil, and he started looking around. It seemed as if there was something very definite he was searching for, the only problem was he had no idea what that something was.

Then his eyes found me, way up towering above him now, and they narrowed.

"Gimme a hand here, feller," he said. He was pretty much whispering.

"What?" I was whispering too. I don't know why.

"Just a little nudge." He looked very serious now. I was scared. "Please, feller?"

But when I reach down and take his hand he yanks hard, pulls me right into him. I felt all his ribs bending under me, like about to crack. You were always feeling Dad's ribs, if you ever got this close. I hated it down here on the floor, but I couldn't tell him because now it was me laughing so hard I couldn't speak. There were a lot of things I wanted to say just then, like so many, but they weren't coming out. That's how hard he was tickling me.

EDUCATION IS OVERRATED

Dad points to the guy, says that's what happens to someone who drinks too much. We were walking out of Jiffy's and in the parking lot we run into this guy. He's in one of those cheap toy-looking pickups, the kind made in Japan or Korea. It was cream-colored, all kinds of dirty, shot up and gnawed at by rust. The guy was in the driver's seat, his head sort of hanging out the window, somewhere right between being asleep and being dead. I think he was Mexican or something. He had that kind of skin, hair so black it looked dyed with ink. I looked real close at him when we passed. His eyelids were shaking.

"*Oops,* feller," Dad says right as I'm looking at him. "Watch out there."

But it's too late. I look down and find my brand new Air Jordans surrounded by a nuclear-green halo of this guy's vomit.

"Don't worry about it," Dad says. "We'll fix 'em up soon as we get back home to Faye's and you'll never know."

I'm too embarrassed to say a thing. No matter what I do for the rest of my life, this actually happened. I could become the President, or some famous movie actor even, and still I couldn't take back that I once stood inside this guy's throw up.

"I'll tell you what that was," Dad says once we're in the car. The tone of his voice is funny, adultlike, which was rare. "That is what happens to someone who drinks too much."

Then he gets the engine started, and we head over to the drive-thru liquor store.

————

Around this time I couldn't go anywhere without someone telling me about what happens when you drink too much, or do even any drugs at all. This was 1990, still Reagan Time for all practical purposes. The Just Say No Era, the D.A.R.E. Years. You know, when the government did anything they could to turn a million ten-year-olds into drug addicts by the time they hit fourteen. There was that damn television commercial running every three minutes, with the dazed beautiful brown-haired woman that every boy eight and up wanted to get with. You know the one. She's up there on the diving board, in this plain white one-piece, rocking lazily on the end. Her hair's in her face so much you can barely see her eyes. She looks sexy. Then she leaps off, with this sort of ragtag grace. But when the camera zooms away it turns out the pool is empty, nothing but concrete, some wilted leaves. Because that, that right there, is your life on drugs. The part that twisted you up the most was that you'd still make out with her in a heartbeat if you were given the chance.

And the year before there had been this assembly for all the kids at College Gardens Elementary, where a cop came in and told us all about drugs. I remember his uniform, light brown, the left chest all smeared with medals that looked like arcade tokens. You knew this was a man with a mission. His voice was polite and stern, almost accusing. Like he was looking at a bunch of four- to eleven-year-olds sitting Indian style, in red-and-orange Jamms knee-shorts, the girls with those jelly sandals suctioned to their feet, convinced *we* were the ones peddling heroin—at *recess*. He told us all about how drugs were evil, evil as anything, the root of all evil. Evil with a capital E.

I felt smarter than everybody else because I already knew this. See, me and Dad had seen this one movie—another that he told me not to tell Mom about—where a bunch of pretty, tan-skinned women in skirts go into the bathroom after getting off some plane. In the stalls they pulled these little plastic balls out from between their legs. The camera kept cutting back and forth between shots of their faces, all grimaced and sweaty, and close-ups of these little balls coming out from between their legs, all shining and dripping. You could tell there was something wrong, but I was still so confused. Then Dad explained that one way they got drugs into America was by putting them into condoms, tying them off, sticking them inside the women. The same place where babies came from, is how he put it. I still had no idea what a condom was, but didn't bother asking.

When the cop finally finished his sermon that day he passed around this clear plastic case. It was sectioned off into little cubes. Each one held tiny samples of all the drugs he had talked about, labeled with neat little white stickers, black type, the real name of the drug and then what the cop called the street name. It was just like show-and-tell. PCP ("ANGEL DUST"). MARIJUANA ("GRASS," "POT," "WEED"). METHAMPHETAMINE ("SPEED," "CRYSTAL," "CRANK"). Since a lot of the younger kids couldn't really read yet, they just crowded around, scanned the plastic with their little fingers. These were little fingers that in class were learning to make lowercase printed Ys and uppercase cursive Gs, papier-mâché ashtrays, origami geese, pinch pots.

The case wasn't all that different from the incubators in our classrooms, where we watched eggs turn into drowsy-eyed, golden-furred chicks. These little birds that walked around like drunks. Life happening. HEROIN ("SMACK"). CRACK ("ROCK"). COCAINE ("BLOW"). Be careful: Life could *un*happen, too.

And then there was Mom, who was also pretty into making sure I knew about drugs. It was actually that same day the cop came to the school that she first mentioned them. I started telling you about this, before I got all side-tracked.

It was like this: I walk home from the bus stop, go downstairs to say hi to Mom. She'd moved her office, her little graphic design firm, into the house by now: Mom and three other employees drawing up things like company logos all day long. She did this to spend more time with me, but a lot of the time it seemed more like she just wanted to work all the time. Anyway, I go down to say hi, and I don't know what I did, can't remember, but whatever it was ended up getting Mom so angry she starts yelling. You should have seen her. She hardly ever yelled, I want to be clear on that. So when it happened, it was pretty intense. Standing right in front of that blue metal desk, the one with the curved metal handles, going off about Dad, saying—

"Do you know something? Do you? Let me just make sure that you know something, young man. That your father's doing cocaine. Do you hear me? Do you?"

I said nothing, prompting her to continue, making sure I understood completely.

"Your father takes *cocaine*. And he's an *alcoholic*. Do you even understand that? Do you even know what that *means*?"

I didn't bother mentioning the assembly.

"And do you know what kind of *debt* I have?" Mom was saying. "Because of him? Because of your father? Do you think he's ever going to pay child support? Do you?"

But I had nothing to say. I wanted to answer her, really, but I didn't know what either debt or child support was.

"Do you have any clue, young man? Do you?"

I wasn't saying anything. I could hear her fine, and I could even see her talking, right there in front of me, her face red and quaking. But all I was thinking about was Dad and the cocaine, and that movie we saw, and that police officer, and that little plastic case. It all just tightened in on my brain, images too potent to turn into coherent thoughts.

Right there I hated that I'd been given no choice but to have all this crammed into my head. No one ever asked my permission. I mean, you guys could have at least *asked*. When you're a kid, no one ever asks your permission about anything. It's funny. Then you get older, and you end up wasting a lot of time trying to remember exactly what everyone said.

Me and Dad were pulling up to the line now, outside the liquor store. It was this small place on the side of a stripmall. The window was thick plastic, you put your money in this metal drawer, shut it, and when you opened it up again there was liquor inside. The same as bank tellers, or David Copperfield. We went here pretty much every time Dad got off work.

And we played this game most every time. Like this:

"Whadya need partner?" Dad asked. "Bottle of vodka?"

"Umm," I said, scratching my chin all dramatic. "Two. Two bottles, please."

"That'll hold ya?"

"I think so. I don't want to end up like that guy back in the parking lot."

"You're a smart kid," Dad said. He was always telling me how smart I was. "Mind sharin' some with me, or should I get my own?"

I was going to tell him that it was best he pick up his own, but just as I'm about to, this guy comes out of nowhere and starts pounding on the hood of Dad's car. Dad never had a car very long, and was driving this white VW Rabbit then, a little four speed that, with this guy banging on the hood all maniacal, felt like it was made of recycled soda cans. Real cheap ones, too. Not Coke or Pepsi, but RC Cola and Fanta. I was nervous. He'd hit the hood and I could feel it in my seat. It was the closest I'd ever come to being in a car wreck. And we weren't even moving.

He was tall, this guy, and, like everybody else in Landover but Dad, he was black. And strong-as-hell-looking. It was already dark out but he still wore mirrored sunglasses. He had on a blue leather trench coat. All of his teeth were gold, and he was so upset with Dad, really pounding on the hood now, and yelling—

"Whatha fuck you doin'? Whatha fuck you doin'?"

"He doesn't look very happy," Dad said to me, all calm.

"Whatha fuck you doin'? Whatha fuck?"

"People are crazy in this neighborhood," Dad told me.

"What's wrong?" I said.

"You wanna fuck with my car?" the man said.

Dad rolled down the window, leaned out. "What's the problem here?" he asked.

"You fuckin' with my car's the problem."

"Dad? Dad, what's wrong?"

"Everyone in this neighborhood's messed up on drugs, feller," is all he said.

———

Jiffy's Subs & Pizza, where Dad was now working, was this skuzzy rip-off on Jerry's, just stuck in even poorer neighborhoods, dingier stripmalls. Just another prime example of one crappy chain giving birth to an even crappier offspring, fast-food inbreeding, the pizza parlor equivalent of one-eyed sisters with two tails.

So Dad worked at Jiffy's for about three years, until the place went out of business after a guy was shot dead out back. But here's the best part: it wasn't the murder that shut the place down. What happened is the guy who shot him ended up killing himself right afterward, by accident, when he tried to run from the cops by climbing up on the roof, which was nothing but these bright shearing clumps of razor wire. The police informed Dad that the amount of razor wire up on the roof was against the law, not in accordance with some code. The place would have to be shut down. That's the kind of luck that never leaves Dad alone.

But until all that, Dad had the manager job again. He had the office with the fake wood walls, the plastic bags with the thick zippers and padlocks. He got to count the money, and, far as I know, he was counting it right this time around.

He seemed happier, but God I hated Landover, the neighborhood where Jiffy's was. It was just east of Rockville and I hated how it smelled, how there was trash everywhere, how the one time I walked somewhere alone three kids circled around me and poured my own Coke over my head.

And I was getting to know Landover well, because Uncle Ray was about to get his divorce from Aunt Edie, and, to give them their space, Dad moved out of their house and into this Landover apartment with Faye, this lady who I swear to you was flat-out crazy. This was the beginning of a trend: shit would explode in Ray's life, Dad would have to move out temporarily. And with Dad the only places he seemed capable of finding were ones already inhabited by some crazy woman.

I think Faye and Dad met at Jiffy's, but I don't know. I never really knew how Dad met the women he did, never really cared. Faye was like a mannequin in almost every way—from her smooth, bright skin, her tight little mouth, her almost invisible eyebrows, her cocked hips—except that Faye was black, and back then there was no such thing as a black mannequin, far as I knew. And I don't joke when I say her apartment was in the projects, raw hallways smelling like urine, empty dime bags in the vestibule, neighbors beating each other up at all hours. It was a very tense place, especially after spending most of the week at Mom's. Her house was feeling more like a mansion each year, without her having to add even one room.

But whenever I would say anything skeptical about Faye, something about how I didn't really like her, Dad would bring up her body. You should see her without clothes, he said, as if offering her to me for a night. You should see the things she can do. I never really got this until this one time I walked in on them together. It was funny. I mean him so pale and her so dark, and God knows where her other leg was, or why she was using that language if she actually *liked* Dad, but still, it made enough sense.

She had these two kittens, named Ollie and Ollie Two. I thought they were named after the skateboarding trick, the one I could never manage to pull off, where you kicked the back of the board into the pavement in order to jump. But it turned out they were named after Oliver North. At the time this meant nothing to me. I remember when I realized how peculiar this was, that this sort of crazed black lady living in this violent apartment building named her kittens after Oliver North. I mean, I *still* barely know who the hell Oliver North is. Do you?

Faye was also always screaming. Sometimes it was magnificent, most of the time just loud and annoying. Everything that came out of her mouth was earsplitting and scratchy. She'd scream hello at you, scream where are my keys at you, scream at the television any time it was on. She drove one of those Nissan 280Zs, the kind that talked to you, told you in this feminine robotic voice that the right door was ajar, the trunk was open, stuff like that. She yelled back at it. I know my door's open! Who do you think opened the damn trunk! How about you try saying shut the hell up!

It was always so odd to me, this constant battery of yelling. But right now, with this man going off on me and Dad, it was starting to make sense. I was thinking it was maybe just a Landover thing. I mean, this guy was really going at it still, yelling—

"Do you not fuckin' hear me? You *deaf* in there? Do you not fuckin' *hear* me?"

"This is a funny place, huh?" Dad said to me.

Dad opened the door now and stepped out. I looked at the guy's car. It was a maroon Camaro or Thunderbird, one of those with the T-top roofs and the plastic slits running down the back window, all the stuff meant for teasing desperate women into thinking they're getting in a Ferrari.

"Whytha fuck you tryin' to hit my car?" the man was yelling at Dad, right up in his face now, so much taller that Dad's mouth was right up level with his Adam's apple, which was convulsing like it was possessed.

He reached past Dad, slammed his fist into the hood again.

"Listen here—"

"Listen to nothin'," the man said. "You tryin' to drive right *into* my fuckin' car."

"Look," Dad said. "I'm at least two feet from your bumper."

"Fuck that."

"Look right there. . . ."

The guy didn't even bother looking, but even I could tell from inside the car that Dad was right. I could even see the guy's bumper, which meant we were nowhere near running into it. Not to mention we weren't even moving.

He took off his sunglasses now, looked right into Dad. God his eyes were huge, perfectly round, all backlit with mayhem.

"Fuck that," he said. "You fuck with my car again you don't even wanna *know* what's gonna happen."

I could not figure out why this man was so convinced we were trying to drive into the back of his car. The cop never mentioned this as a side effect of drugs. It made no sense to me, but still, there did seem a high chance that this guy was going to kill Dad. You could tell he was certainly interested, that he had it in him, that he'd do it and only realize later, like the next day, what he'd done. And he still wouldn't mind, even then. But Dad was so relaxed, like he was talking to anyone. That's the thing with Dad. He's always so relaxed. I guess people who get used to being the one who messed things up have trouble ever getting that angry. I guess they always feel too pathetic placing blame.

"Okay, okay," Dad was now saying.

"Okay nothin'. Get in your car and back the fuck up."

"All right," Dad said. "Sure thing."

"Whytha fuck you tryin' to hit me in the first place?"

"All right," Dad said again. "All right."

When Dad turned around to walk back toward the car, the guy slammed his fists down on the hood one more time. I felt it rattle all through the car, all up through my seat, up through me, pulling at my bones, like someone wanted me cut in two. I took a deep breath, like I had to make sure I could still breathe. He left some dents but that didn't really matter, because that Rabbit was already more dents than smooth surfaces.

When Dad came in he lit a Vantage, pulled on it, looked at me and grinned. There was a part of me that wanted to ask for a cigarette, to prove something. I don't know what.

"Neighborhood's always good for a little adventure, huh, feller?" Dad said. He was always so pragmatic. He put the car in reverse, gave the man his space.

"You weren't even close to his car," I said.

"Half the people in this neighborhood are all messed up on drugs," Dad said again. "Take the right drugs, and every car you see is tryin' to run you over."

It was strange getting drug lessons from Dad, but I just nodded. I never brought up that I knew he was messed up on drugs too. That way he was like a secret experiment of mine. I could use Dad to test out things people like that cop and Mom told me about drugs, and the things they do. It was sort of confusing though, because Dad never once acted like any of the screwed up people we watched in the videos. Dad wasn't black, wasn't living in the streets like them. Dad seemed smart enough. Dad never said anyone was trying to run him over. I mean, Dad never dove into any empty swimming pools.

He still hasn't.

BELATED THANK-YOU NOTE

When Cousin Mike came in and started freaking out, me and Dad were watching *Beverly Hills 90210*. Uncle Ray was through getting divorced with Aunt Edie at this point, had moved into this house in a nearby Rockville suburb that none of us really knew existed beforehand. This meant that after something like two ridiculous years, Dad could finally end things with Faye, which is exactly what happened. So he was living with his brother again, no wives to worry about, a couple of too-old bachelors, Dad thirty-four, Ray forty. You should have seen their fridge. It was always empty but for at least two boxes of pink wine.

The neighborhood was one of these mid-seventies suburbs. One-story look-alike homes of wood and moldy aluminum, small driveways leading to clapboard carports, cul-de-sacs framed by scraggly dogwoods. People's initials were carved into the sidewalk. It was the type of place where married American families had once lived, where kids like me were conceived, but had now given way to ambitious Koreans and Indians, these very polite families that kept to themselves. If you weren't an immigrant in this neighborhood you were a divorced Jew, and if you weren't a divorced Jew you were Ray and Dad, two pale half-assed Catholics from a farm up in Maine with permanent five o'clock shadows, who were divorced *from* Jewish women.

Everything about the house was tweaked, somehow off. The carpets, a sort of industrial blue-gray, were stained when Ray bought the house. Like bruised bruises, and no one ever seemed to entertain the idea of cleaning them. It had a funny smell too, subtle and acrid, as if in some undiscovered alcove there was something rotting. There was hardly any furniture, all of it secondhand, leftovers from Ray's divorce. In the living room there were two pink pleather loveseats, made even uglier with platinum vinyl piping. The dining room table, tusk-white plastic covered unevenly in dime-sized teal polka dots, was too scary to eat at. Basically, Ray got all the stuff that epitomized mid-eighties JAP cheekiness to such an extent that even Edie was embarrassed to hold on to it. And let me point out to you here that Edie, with her frosted gold-brown hair, her gargantuan gold-brown sunglasses, her treasured gold-brown leather blouses, her cubic-zirconium smile and LeBaron convertible, was the local representative of the American JAP circa 1985.

Even the towels in the house were funny. They were so starched they sort of felt like damp cardboard when you were drying off, like rub too hard and they'll disintegrate. None of them matched, all were covered in the logos from the various hotels from which Ray stole them on business trips. The silverware was equally mismatched, and for the same reason: every time Ray and Dad went out to eat they'd swipe the silverware, pulling it out of their pockets on the way to the car, laughing until their faces were all splotched with red. Over the years they had acquired enough to accommodate an enormous family feast, Thanksgiving for a thousand. The only problem was that no one really had much of a family anymore. This was not a bad thing. It just ended up meaning we didn't have to do the dishes very often.

All I cared about were two things. That Dad was done with Faye, because spending even just two days a week at that apartment of hers never got to feeling normal. And that he still had that waterbed mattress. And he had his own room now, like a legit bedroom, his first really since I'd known him, with a television, which right now was tuned into *Beverly Hills 90210*. This was early on, 1993, before the whole cast was jumping into bed with each other, when it was just Brenda and Brandon trying to cope with how difficult it was to live someplace where there were no real problems.

Then Mike comes in, and it was so funny how he just lost it. All when Dad asked—

"So, whadya boys think we should do about dinner?"

Mike's quiet at first, just sort of looks at me and Dad like he doesn't know who we are. Like why are you guys in this room in my house? And then, suddenly, his whole face just rips wide open and he starts crying, like someone had just sprayed tear gas all over the room. It was the oddest thing. Me and Dad turned away from the television completely and just watched him. Mike kept on trying to speak, but kept on choking on himself, on his own words.

"What's up, feller?" Dad said.

"What's wrong?" I asked.

"Mike?"

"You okay, Mike?"

"Everything fine?" Dad asked.

But Mike didn't seem too interested in providing an answer, not just yet. He just kept on shaking. I mean really shaking. He was doing that thing where people can't look any more pathetic, that thing where their mothers are the only people in the world who won't look away in shame. But the thing was, Mike's mother was Edie, and she decided long ago to look away, permanently. He was trying to say something, but it was all clogged up, plunged far down inside him, and still expanding. Me and Dad just watched, intent, like it was some movie we'd paid for and were now regretting. We looked at each other, hoping the other would have something to say, know what to do.

———

Mike was such a smooth, lanky kid. He had these big, confused brown eyes, cowlicked hair the same color. The kid wet his bed until he was ten, sucked his thumb until Ray decided it was best to coat it in some rancid poison, so if he went at the thumb in his sleep this foul taste would bite at the inside of his mouth, hijack his dreams, turn them into nightmares, wake him up and remind him just how stupid he was for sucking his thumb in the first place. By the time he kicked the habit, he was stuck with these screwed up bright-blue teeth, ended up having to be put in headgear, this purple rubberband muzzle pulling his face in ten thousand directions, worn in the day, not at night, like punishment, postponing his chances of ever getting a girl even to smile at him for at least three years. He also had these big, disclike ears, jutting straight out of his head like some NASA prototype. When he hit thirteen Edie forced him to get plastic surgery, to pin them back. That's the kind of mom Edie was—she had to fix him up so she could stand looking at him when she had company.

During those four years Dad lived with Ray, Dad only got me Wednesday nights and every other weekend. Mom had cut down my time with him. Anyway, me and Mike hung out all the time. We could do pretty much whatever we wanted, because our parents were either working, laughing so hard they couldn't see, or passed out. The best part of the house was that it faced out onto this enormous field, acres and acres of flat earth leftover from when Maryland was a mill state, from when D.C. was a nothing city fizzing out into nothing country. Not that it was of historic significance to me and Mike. We played football back here, walkie-talkie spy games, crabapple baseball, freeze tag. We were also into peeping on this one fat neighbor showering, and other petty delinquent shit, like reading people's mail or sneaking into unlocked cars, stealing the cigarette lighters, then putting them back an hour later.

Since I had a year on him, I was the faster one and the stronger one, the smarter one and the less clumsy one. Because Ray was that kind of dad, a man who valued the Redskins and the bench press above all else, he'd often point this out to Mike when we were together, how compared to me he was basically nothing, scrawnier than an anorexic pigeon is how he put it more than once. And I had put on some weight finally, it's true, but I was no linebacker. Still, back then Ray's chief philosophical question in life was, essentially: Why the fuck could his son not be more like me?

But there was this one time when I wasn't the boss with Mike, and, because I'm into trying to be honest with you, I think it should be pointed out here. We were playing in the woods this one time, and came up on a rattlesnake. Being around twelve, the only thing that made sense was to start peeing on the thing. You know, just to see what would happen. So there we are, pissing on this rattlesnake, and I look over and see Mike's got hair, thin and brown and all burnt looking, where I still had none. And I was older. Not that he knew I was freaking out, not that he knew he could have had the upper hand. I've always been pretty good like that, and anyway, Mike ended up slipping on some rock, falling, and pissing all over his chin. If you can even picture that.

———

Finally, Mike's still crying all hysterically, but some words are getting out now.

It comes in these snotty, erratic sentences that take a while to make sense. He was saying something about his dad, about Ray, who was out of the house right now, giving the Bronco an oil change. He starts really making sense, these hot fragments finding orbit, Mike saying—

"He . . . he, he'll be chasing me around the house, yelling. He'll be yelling I'll . . . I'll fucking *kill* you. I'm gonna . . . *get* you."

"Mike—" Dad said.

"He's like . . . you can't hide from me," Mike went on. "One time I . . . I . . . I ran all through the house. And had . . . I had to *hide* behind Mommy. . . ."

It was funny hearing the word mommy, sort of pathetic, but I didn't think this was the time to bring it up.

"I was behind her, and he, Dad, was trying to get me," Mike was saying. "Mom was like, get away, get away, I hate you so much. But, but . . . he . . . he's always trying to *hit* me. He, he . . . God I *hate* him so much."

———

The only woman who would ever be impressed by a house like Ray's was one begging to be impressed by something, anything, please. Fortunately for Ray, and for Dad, these women were everywhere back then. They'd come out of some marriage and straight into our house, like it was the law. I remember Anne, who had such monstrous golden curls that it was impossible to tell the actual length of her hair. It was also, because of the lost, lighthearted way she moved around, impossible to determine who had met her first, Dad or Ray. And there was Peg, who couldn't go to the bathroom without ever crying, and Melinda and Jane and Beth, this lady who was always using one of those lame paper pinch puppets—cootie catchers, she called them—to tell me and Mike our futures. Now lift up that flap right there, and look: you'll be married with four kids! These women never lived with us very long, only a week or so. But that didn't stop Mike, the resident expert at messing up, from slipping up a few times and calling a couple of them mom.

But hearing him now, it didn't seem like such a big mistake—

Oh you should have seen these tears! His face was all shredded up, like it wasn't tears he was crying, but sand, *pulverized glass.* And the things Mike started to say. He was talking about his sister now, Stacey, and how there was this one time, or maybe lots of times, where Ray had her pinned down on the kitchen floor, which was these big linoleum tiles covered in yellow daisies. He held both her wrists in one of his hands, his knees pressing down on the tops of her thighs. She was in a T-shirt, and underwear, and those floppy teenage-girl socks. Mike was telling me and Dad how Ray was calling her a fucking bitch, a slut. He was slapping her too, right across the face, using both sides of his hand. Stacey was fifteen, and suddenly it made so much sense to me why she was hardly ever around, why the only time you'd ever see her she'd be getting into some twenty-year-old guy's car, like come on, let's get out of here . . . *Now!*

It keeps on, for fifteen minutes at least—

"At night, he, he . . . I hate him, I really *hate* him. His face gets so red. He'll be screaming, he screams, and . . . and . . . and I'll have *bruises.*"

"Hey there, Mike—"

"He . . . he . . . he's been doing it for like . . . *forever.*"

Mike said his friends would sometimes ask about the bruises. Like what's that? How'd you get that? Mike said this happened lots of times, and that he never knew what to say. It struck me that I should have noticed these bruises, all the times we were together, but somehow I never did. Me and Dad just looked at him, waiting for him to stop because then we could figure out if any of this was really happening or not. We just had no idea what to do, me and Dad. Because I was young, and because for Dad it was family, and he had no clue about family.

————

The last year Ray lived there, some construction company bought the field in the back of the house, to turn it into one of these crammed developments. You know, the kind that in the nineties seemed to fill every last piece of open grass in this country. You may be living in one right now, for all I know. They were these huge houses, brick facades but aluminum sides, mansions I guess, but pressed so close together you could tell there was something wrong. They may as well have been tenements. I mean, you could easily tie laundry lines up between them. I think some people even did.

But that's not the point. The point is that me and Mike had to start playing in the construction sites. It was the only thing that made sense. We'd play war games in the foundations, play king of the hill on the bulldozers, tour the homes when they were nothing but sandbags and wood frames and pink insulation. And all I'm saying is that the one time I decided to stay inside was the day the cops knocked on our door and informed Ray that they'd found Mike creeping around back there. That's trespassing, the cops said, which was against the law. Ray apologized very professionally. He told the cops that he'd take care of it, if they didn't mind. He said that he knew his son, said he knew him well.

Ray said he knew just what to do—

"Hey Brenda, something up?" I heard Brandon saying to his sister on television. Mike was still talking but I was having trouble listening.

"I'm just worried," Brenda said, "about Dylan. He's been drinking again."

"How about I take you for a milkshake?" Brandon suggested. "At the Peach Pit."

"I hate him so much," Mike was now saying. His words were still all minced and burning, but finding order. He took a breath. "I really hate him so much. I'm not even joking," he said.

"The Peach Pit sounds perfect," Brenda said.

"Mike?"

"I want to kill him," he said. "I wish he was dead."

———

Mom's all like, my God, oh my God, I can't believe it.

"I know," I was saying. "I know."

"That's really *Mike?*" she said. "I can't believe it."

This was just this year, just a few months ago, me twenty years old now. I was home for Christmas, or Hanukkah—it's never mattered to us. Grammy, my grandmother on Dad's side, sent me this card. I haven't seen her in years, so it was good to know she's still alive. Anyway, there's a photo inside, a picture of Mike, first I'd seen of him in years. Me and Mom, staring at it, we couldn't get over it.

"I mean, I knew he got messed up," Mom was saying, "but this is just—"

"Yeah," is all I could say. "Yeah . . ."

You should have seen it. There's Mike, tall and strong—actually *beautiful*. His head's shaved, his skin tan. He's graduating from the military of all places, shaking some general's hand. I didn't bother mentioning that when I looked at this photo I remembered one time, a while ago, when Dad asked about dinner and that kid went off about how his father was always trying to kill him. It didn't matter now, because it wasn't even Mike anymore. Me and Mom just stood there, looking at this picture, at this stranger in it, and right there I should have said something to Mom, but I didn't. I just should have told her thanks. Thank you so much, because I'd be that kid if you were a million different women.

CUT UP, NO BLOOD

ONE

Snow slanting down in sheets, really freezing out, the kind of Northeastern cold that turns your face to solid ice, then takes out a chisel and starts picking away. And the walk over to her house, to Claudia's, it takes forever. You go right out of my house, down Nelson Street, left on College Parkway—which isn't really a parkway of any sort, just a two-lane street bordered by townhouses and tract houses all done up in these earthy shades of tan, beige, bleached yellow. You take this all the way past College Gardens Elementary, until it ends at College Plaza. Now cut through the parking lot, past the Shoppers Food Warehouse, the Kwick Stop, the Trak Auto, the Kentucky Fried Chicken, and every other place popular with people who never even think about college. So now you're on Route 355, Rockville Pike, a six-lane trench protected by the type of wide variety of stripmall architecture essential for a lifetime of loitering. But this part of the Pike you're on now, it's a little north of all that. This is the Jiffy Lube section, the used-car parking-lot stretch, the neon print in the windshield portion. The signs are in Spanish and English. It's the part leading up to the Gude Drive overpass, and that mean's you're halfway to Claudia's and should therefore quit caring about the fact that you're so cold you can't even blink right.

That's where I was right now, the Gude Drive overpass, a four-lane concrete slab bent over the Metro tracks, the Red Line, straight to the senators of D.C. in thirty minutes, to the crack houses in thirty-five. There's a thick concrete median, tall chain-link fences on either side, curving in at their tops like uncut fingernails. You know, like making sure no one ever jumps. The road was covered in dirty snow, slushed-out tire tracks crisscrossing as if two hideous skiers had just shot past. I hated it here, up on the overpass, because for some reason having to do with physics I'll never comprehend, it was always freezing up here. Like up here, it gets cold even in hot weather.

After the overpass you go by Montgomery Donuts, which is connected to some sort of auto shop, the outside smelling like burned rubber and recycled WD-40, and where the blueberry-crunch donuts are about ten times superior to the ones at Dunkin's. Now it's left on some road you never knew the name of, a new road—laid down just yesterday, you swear. And then take a right into the Hollybroke development, which went up in twenty minutes a year ago, filled up with assimilating immigrants in forty-five seconds. This means you're now officially out of Rockville, into Derwood, and so close to her house that you're already tasting that watermelon Bubble Yum on her tongue.

It was that taste, all sandy-sweet, that was wrapped around my mind as I pushed the doorbell, pressed my face against the brushed glass window. And there's Claudia, just look at her: here she comes, just a dim blur behind the glass, coming up to the door. She opened it, and I saw her mother standing right there over her shoulder. This meant I could not start kissing Claudia immediately and would have to come up with something cunning to say, something really genius, which ended up being—

"Oh my God, it's so cold out there."

Not that I wasn't wearing enough layers. I was taking off my jackets now, piling them up in front of the door, first a little nothing windbreaker, now one of those Columbia parkas, the kind everyone had to have, even though the detachable fleece liners only came in gay blinding blue or even gayer blinding pink. Over that I was sporting a hooded Pittsburgh Pirates Starter jacket, total wigger style, that belonged to an old best friend at the time, this good kid Jamie who I fell out of touch with that September, right when high school happened. You know, because it's practically mandatory that you lose all your friends when high school starts. I haven't talked to him in years. Last I heard he was in Austin, busing tables at T.G.I. Friday's, subsisting on thirty joints a day. It's pretty funny, how Rockville's this decent town, but every kid I knew who grew up there is living some life like this. I still have Jamie's jacket, though, stuffed in the back of some closet, which is all I really wanted to mention. You'll see why in a minute.

Sixth and seventh grade I was petrified of girls. They'd talk to me sometimes, say these confusing things like Hi, or Hey, hand me intricately folded notes asking How r u? Or Wuz up, down, all around? Like the better they got at English the smarter they got at messing it up. In the sixth grade these paralyzing moments came during the fifteen-minute break we got after lunch, where we were supposed to be thinking about the soldiers in Desert Storm, but really just walked around the Julius West Middle School parking lot staring at our feet.

In the seventh grade it was in the hallways at the end of the day, or outside as the buses pulled up. Every time I'd just stand there, look at them like a dumb-ass, these girls in clip-on earrings, their training bras bunched up under T-shirts, lips all smeared with the first touches of lipstick, stonewashed jeans severely cuffed at the bottom. I remember Carla, the girl from Uruguay or Paraguay, one of those, always chewing an eraser, spandex booty shorts riding up her ass like they were trying to exit out her mouth. Or Nanja, the black girl, first one in the grade with breasts, that Heavy D T-shirt stretched so tight the rapper looked twice as fat as he already was. Or Julie, white and Jewish, her bangs coated in so much hairspray they looked like a Slinky. But I'd just look at them, these girls, wait for them to go away, disappear, because that's when I'd get my voice back, be able to say something.

But when the eighth grade came around something happened. I hit thirteen, certain chemical reactions occurred, adding a few inches, giving me a voice no longer higher than the girls', pulling my face into the kind of shape I didn't mind looking at in the mirror anymore. Nirvana was the band to listen to then, in 1993, so I was dressing like a Gap version of Kurt Cobain: the unbuttoned flannel, baggy construction-worker jeans, the kind with the little loop no one ever knew was really for a hammer, black Doc Marten boots scrubbed with sandpaper to look ten years old instead of brand new. I don't mean to sound like I'm bragging, but somehow with all this came an ability to talk to girls, which is how I got to know Claudia, and which is probably the reason I don't know why that Gude Drive overpass is so damn windy all the time. Because once I started talking to them, I quit paying attention to school for a long time.

———

Claudia was putting in a CD right now. It was the Spin Doctors. God, I hated the Spin Doctors, right up there with 4 Non Blondes, Cracker, and Soul Asylum—Claudia's other favorite bands. Not that I was about to say anything. I've always been into keeping small secrets like that from women, the kind that the older you get start to come off a whole lot like flat-out lies. I don't know. Women always seem to get so angry when you tell the truth, or maybe it's that I haven't figured out what telling the truth means. But whatever: None of it makes me proud. I'm trying to stop.

Like all the homes that everyone I knew lived in, Claudia's had two living rooms, one that was always a demolition zone, Sega Genesis controllers knotted up in front of the television, Costco-sized Pepperidge Farm cookie boxes everywhere, about fifty remotes stuck to the coffee table because of a glass of Hawaiian Punch that spilled four years ago. This was where everyone was half the time, Claudia's two little brothers pulling out each other's hair, her younger sister pulling the fat on her waist and frowning, her mother glued to some soap opera or talk show, like it could actually tell her something important about the world.

Then there was the other living room that no one ever went in. That's where me and Claudia were right now, where we always were. It sort of looked like a furniture store display, all done up in a creamy off-white: stiff off-white couches, a matching carpet, off-white ceramic knick-knacks in an off-white glassed-panel knickknack cabinet. Even the stereo was off-white. Since her family had moved from Peru a few years ago, this all had that especially trying quality of an immigrant family trying to figure out what American means.

"Would he like some chocolate hot?" her mother was now yelling from the kitchen, just around the corner.

"You mean *hot chocolate*," Claudia said. She was always teaching her mom how to speak English right, even though her accent was pretty thick too.

"Would he like some?"

"Mom, I bet he can hear you fine, considering he's *right here next to me*. Why don't you come in and *ask* him?"

Now her mom said something in Spanish, and Claudia looked at me and smiled, then said something back in Spanish. I'm no linguist, but I figured out quick that her mother would be coming around the corner in due time with two mugs of hot chocolate.

"Your mom's funny," I said. I was always noticing people's moms back then, never their dads. I guess the more I lived only with Mom, the more I didn't think of dads as really mattering. Claudia had a dad though, this guy who was around and always hated me for liking his daughter. But this didn't matter. Like I said, I never noticed people's dads.

"She's so annoying," Claudia was saying.

Claudia was wearing the standard uniform of freshman girls' milling around the house: radioactive-orange Umbros, the seams atrophied, a long-sleeved T-shirt with something on it having to do with some beach no one's ever really been to. Her hair, straight black down to her shoulders, was pulled back in a purple scrunchie, floppy cotton socks on her feet. The best part were the Umbros, because whenever she shifted into some position that pulled them tight around her hips you'd get a veiled glimpse at her underwear.

This is what was happening right now, as she's on her knees leaning into the stereo to put in the goddamn Spin Doctors. They looked white, and cotton, cut high on the sides. I reached out, put my hand on the back of her thigh, slid it up to just under the taut line of the shorts.

Claudia moves back, knocks my hand away, saying—

"My *mom* is right in there."

—in this whisper, with this grin riding her thin brown lips that did nothing but reinforce the foundation of my erection, which was already stronger than kryptonite. So when, as if on cue, her mother turns the corner, I had to shift quick into a less conspicuous position.

"Oh thank you," I said, taking the glass.

"Welcome," her mother said. "Warmest now?"

"It's warm*er*," Claudia said.

"Yeah," I said. "Getting there. Pretty warmest. Thank you."

Now came this awkward moment that happened every time I came over here, had been happening during the almost whole year I'd been with Claudia. Her mother sits down with us on the couch, and then no one knows what to say. We just sit there, the three of us, sort of half smiling in silence, furiously sipping or eating whatever beverage or snack is present. The couch cushions really were stiff—you suddenly felt that now. And for some reason these moments always tended to occur just as I was getting an erection, so I'd be in that annoying state where you try not to think about it, you know, so it will go away, but then, because you're trying so hard not to think about it, all that happens is it just keeps getting more ridiculous. So there we are, sitting there, waiting for her mother to get up, smile, tell us she'll be in the kitchen, right around the corner, working on the dinner, if we need anything, anything at all.

"It's just *cooking* dinner," Claudia was saying. "God mom! Not *working on* the dinner."

Her mother said something in Spanish, then left the room.

———

"Could you taste the chocolate?" I now asked. Finally, I'd kissed the girl.

"No," she said. "I've been drinking it too."

"I thought you'd taste like Bubble Yum."

"I ran out," she said.

Before Claudia, my experience with kissing wasn't so impressive. That's because it was confined only to those long, glorious make-out sessions with my bathroom mirror. Our first kiss happened during a game of truth or dare, where three orange Tic Tacs traveled from my mouth to hers. These were the anxious, mechanical, pistonlike kisses of kids. But they'd gotten much better, like more liquid, over the past year. And now my braces were off, so we didn't have to worry about the taste of blood getting in the way anymore.

"Can you feel how warm it is?" Claudia was now asking, sort of whispering, her mouth right up to mine. "Because of the hot chocolate?"

"It feels cool," I said. "Let's go for a walk."

"Not yet."

"Why not?"

"Just wait," she said.

"We'll say we're gonna go sledding."

"We don't have any sleds."

"Who doesn't have any *sleds*?" I asked.

"*Us*," she said.

"Then we'll say we're gonna make a snowman."

"Aren't we too old for that?" Claudia asked.

———

We called it the rug, this place we went in the woods behind her house. It was called the rug because after the first few times we went there, I brought this old blanket I had lying around. Brown, nappy as hell, the thing looked like a depressed shag carpet. Not that I'm complaining: it was a lot better for fooling around on than the bare ground, which left us picking small rocks out of our skin, itching from never-cut blades of grass.

We started going back here over the summer, in the afternoons, pawing at each other until one of us had to get home for dinner. We kept the rug in one of those bags used for men's suits. You know, the long plastic kind they give you at fancy stores like Macy's. That way it wouldn't get all screwed up in the rain.

And right now, our feet all crunching in the snow as we walked to the rug, the snow had eased up and I swear it wasn't even cold out anymore. Like all of a sudden. I can't explain it—sometimes my senses just flip on and off, get kind of frantic and go haywire, like they can only deal with so much at once. And right now that meant only Claudia.

It was just very quiet. That's all I'm saying. You could even hear the few flakes falling down on themselves. No sun, no shadows. And feel that: Claudia's breath turning to mist, the wind picking it up, breaking it against my face. You can smell her Chapstick, cherry flavored. It's practically still happening, all of it, happening right this second, if you think about it the right way—

Every house in this neighborhood was white, one-story, all made of aluminum, only two models total. Call it a boring place, but I always liked that kind of order, found it sort of tranquil. There were no cars out, hadn't been for a while, so everything was covered evenly in the snow, the houses practically blending right into the earth. Our footprints were the only things messing this up.

It was a snow day, school canceled for the third day in a row. What I'm saying is that maybe if it were a normal day, if it hadn't been freezing, if it hadn't been an entire three days since we'd last seen each other—well, I bet we would have made it to the rug, as was planned, a ten-minute walk down the path to that little weedy alcove where we kept it.

But that's not what happened.

We were stopped now. Look at us, we're right there:

deep enough into the woods where it no longer feels like someone's neglected backyard, where you no longer see houses squeezing through the slits in the trees. I turn to Claudia like—

"So?"

"Are you cold?" Claudia asks.

"No, are you?"

"Not really."

"Yeah, me neither." I guess I'd already forgotten that I'd just said this. "Do you want to . . . I don't know . . . make a snowman?"

"You have a snowflake on your nose," Claudia's now saying—

It's the same furious, charged, methodical kissing already mentioned, but with an added utilitarian element: it's keeping us warm right now. The harder we kiss, the warmer we get, the heat in our mouths seeping all up through our faces, shattering into our heads, spiking down all through our bodies. My hands go up the back of Claudia's jacket, up under her shirt, the strap of her bra running up under my fingernails. Her back's so smooth, kind of sliding under my hands as she shivers, her vertebrae biting down on itself, spastic because of my cold palms. But she doesn't seem too concerned, and a second later . . . my hands aren't even cold anymore. I take Claudia's hands now, because you had to do a lot of coaxing with Claudia, and I put them up the back of my jacket. It's really crazy. Her hands had been on my cheeks, so they're not cold at all. They almost burn even.

I begin unzipping the outer layer now, that Pirates Starter jacket I was telling you about.

"What are you doing exactly?" Claudia asks.

I don't say anything, a smart enough move, as Claudia's now the one unzipping that gay Columbia parka, now the windbreaker. So you should have seen us. God, it really was tremendous. Just look: we're kneeling now on this sloppy pile of winter coats, both of us in only jeans and sweatshirts, kissing all maniacal.

"God, I'm not cold at all," I now say.

"I know," she says. "Me neither."

"Like I'm even *warm*," I say.

My hands up the front of her shirt now, they go up over her pretty-much-nonexistent breasts, just flip her bra up because I could never figure out that damn clasp. I like them. They're manageable. They were the only breasts I'd ever touched, but already I knew I was the type of man who for whatever reasons is scared of breasts. I just never get what the point of touching them is. I don't know. I think it's that they're just too motherly or something.

So I quickly unzip the front of my pants now, pull them down a bit, encourage the movement of her hand toward the opening of my plaid boxers. Yeah, and now I'm working the button-fly of her jeans. Since she's kneeling, the denim is especially tight around her hips. You know, like each button's a chore.

"Oh my God," I'm now saying. "Do you even know how *warm* you are?"

————

I always liked looking down at my hand, it's movement, at my fingers, how they went away up inside of her. Claudia wasn't so into me looking, said it was too embarrassing. So I'd have to be careful about when I did it. Tact was a must. I'd kiss her neck and take these stealth glances downward. Or sort of make her kiss my neck and do the same thing. But right now she was just kissing my neck on her own, really kissing hard, really into it.

So I decided to look down, at where my hand was. And at first I didn't want to say anything, because Claudia was so crazed and I wasn't really that bothered. But as I kept looking, watching what was happening, I found myself saying—

"Blood."

"What?" Claudia asked, sort of dizzylike, absent-minded, still all up in my neck.

"Blood," I said again. "Blood."

She pulled away, looked down.

"Oh my God," she said.

"There's blood, I know."

"I'm bleeding."

"Are you okay?" I asked.

"Yeah yeah yeah."

"You're bleeding," I said. "Are you fine?"

————

We're both looking down now, at my hand, kind of suspended between us. It was sort of amazing. It was almost entirely covered in blood, very thick and dark and gleaming, thickest around my first two fingers, then sort of streaking down toward my wrist. I mean, there had been that time at the movies, when we went to see *Reality Bites,* that stupid movie about rich kids just out of college trying to fake like they're poor, and in the back corner Claudia was telling me no, that I had to stop, that she was on her period. I said I don't care, like come on, please, wondering was it really that bad, and she went out to the bathroom, threw away her maxi pad, and came back and said okay. If you really want to, it's okay now.

But then there was hardly any at all, just these thin pink-yellow streaks over the tips of my fingers. I didn't really know what to do right now. What's strange is I wasn't really scared, or all that worried, or any less attracted to her. I was just starting to feel the cold again. I was remembering that we were in the middle of the woods, in the snow, sort of half clothed on a pile of jackets. I started feeling funny about the fact that I had this unstoppable erection jetting out from my boxers.

Then Claudia was talking, saying—

"Oh God it's getting on the jacket."

"Oh that's okay," I said. "Don't worry. Don't worry. It's the inside, the lining. And it's not even my jacket anyway."

But I still moved my hand over to the side, wiping it on the snow. It was kind of pretty. We both looked, this solid red against solid white. The snow was absorbing it, spreading it out thin, going from red to pink.

"What are you doing?" Claudia now asked.

I was moving my hand back to her underwear, which, by the way, turned out to be pale blue and not white, and which were all twisted up and bunched right now. There was some hair coming out at the sides.

"I don't know." I said. "It's okay. Is it okay?"

I slip my hand up under the lining now, just rest it there for a moment. It's so warm you don't even know. I kiss her. At first she doesn't kiss me back, but then she does, kisses me real hard and I straighten my fingers and all of me gets warm, warm, really so warm—

Then she bites down on my bottom lip, hard, and then Claudia pulled away.

"What?" I said.

"The snow," she said. "I can feel it. You know, down there."

"Oh," I said. "I'm sorry."

"No, no. It's okay," she said. "I don't know. I kinda like it, if you don't mind."

"No," I said. "Not at all."

I pull my hand away and wipe it in the snow again, in a different place. We watch it dilute again. Then I move back and we're kissing again, hard, just like before. I can feel the snow melting. I start kissing her neck, so I can look down. You can see it on my wrist now, just look: the blood, all mixed up with small pieces of shiny ice. It's getting all over the jacket too, on the bright yellow nylon lining. I don't care at all.

I don't care about anything.

Then she pulls away once more, looks right into me. Right there she looked so honest.

"I think I know what it is," she says. "What just happened. What's happening."

"Is it okay?" I ask.

"Yeah," Claudia says. "It is. It's fine."

TWO

A few weeks before that day with Claudia, the one I just told you about, me and Mom were eating dinner at Boston

Market, that fast food place that I swear is designed for divorced people and their kids—you know, so they can order an eighth of a turkey and string beans and pretend they still have a huge family or something. Me and Mom weren't like this, though. We just loved the butternut squash.

But it was funny that we were eating here right now, I have to say, because I'd just got back from Maine, had gone up with Dad for Thanksgiving, and couldn't shut up about the time I had up there. And now here we were, eating a meal like this. You know, fake Thanksgiving.

"I could never get over how huge his family is," Mom was saying to me.

"I know what you mean," I said.

I wish you could have been up in Maine for one of these Thanksgivings. Since Dad's one of ten kids, and the only one who didn't at least try to have ten of his own, they were really something. All these aunts, uncles, third cousins thrice removed. I was always amazed at how many people there were with the same blood as me who I didn't really know. What was even more amazing is that I just loved them anyway.

"You know who's really great?" I was saying to Mom now.

"Who's that?"

"T.J.," I said. "I spent most of my time hanging out with him."

"You guys are around the same age, right?"

"Not really," I said. "He's twenty-three."

"Jesus . . . ," Mom said. She hadn't seen any of Dad's family in almost ten years, since the divorce obviously, so it made sense that she'd be a little out of it when it came to everyone's age and life story. "I can't believe he's *twenty-three*. I remember when T.J. was younger than you."

T.J. was the oldest of all the cousins, and there was just something glamorous about him. With his almost-black brown eyes, the long lashes, and his black hair and tan skin, he was certainly the best looking person in the family, man or woman. He looked very clean, a lot like the guys you see blown up poster-size in cheap barber shops trying to fake like they're glitzy, places like the Hair Cuttery. And T.J. dressed different from everyone else, real stylish. I admired this. He was living down in Florida, in Fort Myers, waiting tables at the Ritz Carlton. I know this may not sound fancy to you, but in that family it meant he'd got out and hit the big time. I was bussing tables and cleaning the grease trough at this chili restaurant down the street, Hard Times Cafe, so I thought I'd be able to talk the talk, relate to his life. But then T.J.'s telling me about all the *celebrities* he got to serve. People I'd never heard of, like John Ritter. Still, I was impressed as hell. What I liked about it was how adult his life was. I think when you get a father like mine you're especially interested in real adults, you sort of search them out. It's like a hobby. Thing was, talking to T.J., even though he was so grown-up and all, was still pretty much like talking with someone my own age.

"So does he like it in Florida?" Mom was now asking.

"I guess," I said.

"I really can't believe it," she said. "I can't get over how *old* everyone is."

"You know what's weird?" I now said. I'd been thinking about this for a few minutes, ever since we started talking about Dad's family. "I always forget that you actually *know* these people too," I said.

"What do you mean?" Mom said.

"I don't know," I said. "I mean, I know you went up there a lot, like when you and Dad were married, but—"

"We went up with you too," Mom said.

"I know," I said, "but it's not like I can remember that."

"Not at all?" Mom asked. She almost sounded upset by this. "Seriously?"

"Nope," I said. I wasn't going to lie to her. Mom's the one person I'd never lie to. "Nothing."

Mom had this odd look running all over her face right now. I'd seen this before. It was the same look she'd get when we talked about Opa, my grandfather, the one who died about ten minutes before Mom and Dad split up, in 1987. She'd go on and on about Opa and I'd just sit there, then say Mom, I don't remember any of that, I only remember him in the hospital. It always blew her away that there were these things between us, different spaces in our lives that were filled with the same material, filled with people like Opa and Dad. You know, things that affected both of us, but just in completely opposite ways.

Later on, when I'd be a little older, and Mom would get this look—a sort of depressed but resilient look—I'd just think wow, this lady has been through it. I'd think about my friends' mothers, how they always seemed ready to break apart, dissolve completely, and I'd wonder how does mine do it? She'd impress me, and in time I learned to say something to her, give her props for being such a cool lady. But when I was thirteen I didn't really get any of that. Truth is, back then, whenever she got this look I just got uncomfortable, annoyed even.

So I went back to the subject at hand—

"Yeah . . . ," I said. "T.J. *is* pretty cool. He really is."

I was hoping this would maybe bring us back to a kind of normal conversation. But then, I swear out of nowhere, Mom's asking—

"Why don't we go up?"

"What's that?"

"To Maine," she said. "Why don't we go up, for Christmas?"

I had absolutely no idea what I was supposed to do with this.

"Um . . . ," I said. Then I didn't say anything for a second. I just ate my squash. "Um . . . sure," I said. "I mean, I guess so."

"Just the two of us," Mom was saying. "Your father's staying down here at Ray's for the holidays, so it won't be a problem."

I was getting more into the idea now, I admit. I mean, if you had seen Mom right there, how excited she looked, you would have been into it too, even if it was pretty bizarre.

————

So there we were, a few weeks later, me and Mom, driving up from Maryland to spend Christmas with Dad's family, twelve hours of watching 95 North get less and less polluted with traffic. It was a better car ride than the one a month before with Dad, I'll tell you, because that's when he had his VW bus, when he had gone on and on about Shirley, that lady who lived with us when I was a kid, and about her inheritance, about the cocaine.

It was hysterical, how it all came up. I was like—

"So, how much longer till we're there?"

—and Dad somehow manages to take this as a secret cue for him to start in on Shirley.

"Hey," he said, "you remember Shirley? Lived with us when me and your mother were married?"

"Yeah," I said. "Well, sort of."

"She was a crazy girl . . . ," he said. It was funny, the way

Dad was talking, all whimsical. It was obvious he wanted me to ask about her. When I think about it, Dad used me as a kind of confessional a lot back then.

"What do you mean?" I was thirteen, so of course I had to ask.

So Dad goes on and on, telling me about some party, about Shirley dancing half naked up on some table. She was an ex-Playmate, he says. Did you know that? You should have seen her breasts, so beautiful. I was old enough to grasp that Dad shouldn't be telling these sorts of details, shouldn't be telling me any of it actually, but it's not like this upset me, if you can get that. I just kind of nodded, thinking if Dad wants to tell me all this that's fine. What can I really do?

But there was one problem. I wanted to ask him about the cocaine, get some of the specifics, because all I really knew was what Mom told me that one time, and she was more screaming it for her own good than mine. Really I just wanted to know whether or not he'd stopped taking it yet. But the thing was, Dad never said straight out that he was doing it too. The guy was actually convinced I'd believe he was just there, around the cocaine, watching Shirley up on the table, all innocent. See, that's the problem with people like Dad. They try to confess something to you, something that might actually matter, but they just end up telling another lie.

Anyway, Mom's graphic design business was doing well now, like she was sort of on her way to rich, so I guess what happened up in Maine makes sense, just knowing Mom.

Me, Mom, and T.J. are sitting around baking Christmas cookies, and when she sees the careful attention T.J. pays to the designs on the cookies—the smoothing of the icing, the precise placement of the sprinkles and those little silver balls you never knew if you were supposed to eat or not—she asks him have you ever considered going into design. T.J. says he has actually, never very seriously, but yeah, he has.

"I bet you'd be good at it," Mom said.

And, to make a long story short, a few weeks later T.J.'s quit his job as a waiter. He's packed up his red Chevy Beretta and moved to Maryland, to work for Mom, in her office in the basement. He was living with us, with me and Mom, sleeping on the couch.

I liked this for a lot of reasons. Of course because T.J. was so cool and adult, but the main one being that he wore a lot of suits, which was funny because he was just working downstairs. But T.J. was very into looking professional, it was a serious matter with him. Not that I cared. His wearing suits is how me and Claudia got that plastic bag where we kept the rug, so the rain wouldn't get to it. I also liked him living with us because I could ask him certain questions, things that before just stayed in my head and drove me sort of mad, like right now when I was saying to him—

"And she said she knew what it was, that it was okay, and that was pretty much it. But I never asked what it was."

T.J. starts laughing. We were in my bathroom, like we were every night, in boxers and T-shirts, bushing our teeth, washing our faces. T.J. would often criticize my hygiene, say I didn't floss enough, say I wasn't clean. Like wearing the suits, that was one of his quirks: the whole concept of *clean* was very important to him, he'd talk about it the way people talk about the President, or the love lives of movie stars, another topic T.J. was really into.

But most of the time we just talked about Claudia. It was funny. T.J. was actually the one who started these little chats. He always seemed to especially like hearing the details of me and Claudia, even though I was only fourteen now and he'd probably done everything I was talking about ten times over.

"What?" I said. "What's so funny?"

"You really don't know what happened?"

"No. What was it?"

He's laughing again, then brushing his teeth, real hard, then spitting in the sink.

"Okay," he said. "Do you know what the word hymen means?"

"No."

"What about cherry?" T.J. asked. "Do you know what I mean when I say cherry?"

Now I was spitting in the sink.

"Do you?"

"Sure," I said, wiping my mouth. "I mean, sort of."

But T.J. saw I had no idea, so he sort of laughed again and then explained, about virginity, and how what happened with me and Claudia that afternoon wasn't how it normally happened, but that she was right, everything was okay. I was so intrigued. Around this time there were a lot of these moments, with people like T.J., or even just kids my age, where I'd be talking to someone and it would just hit me, in this sour fragmented way, that there were a lot of things I should have known about already, but didn't, just because I lived only with Mom.

"I can't believe you guys were outside," he was now saying.

"I know," I said.

"In the *snow*," he said.

"Yeah. I know."

"Gives you something to think about in the bathroom," T.J. now said.

It was funny, how he suddenly looked very excited saying this. I just looked at him, at his face in the mirror. Like for a second there he was speaking to someone else, and I was waiting for him to get back to me.

I guess he was seeing this expression on my face, because he was suddenly all joking, but sort of smirking too, like—

"Oh, you *know* you do it! Come on!"

Look, I understood what he was talking about. It's not like I was five or something. And this conversation had occurred before. But the thing was, if you need to know, I actually never had done it before, touched myself, even though I was fourteen. I don't mean to brag, but I was in the rare position of having a girl doing it to me at the exact time I would have started doing it myself.

But I didn't really get that then, and the topic made me sort of jittery. I didn't really feel like deconstructing it right then. That's why I just smiled all awkward at T.J. in the mirror and said—

"I swear I don't."

"Oh come on!"

"I don't."

"Give me a *break*," T.J. said. He almost sounded a little pissed off now. "*Every*body does it."

I never could figure out why T.J. was so entranced with the subject, why he was always bringing it up, wanted me to admit it so badly. In the few months he'd lived with us, this came up many times. Like every week actually. It was one of the few things I didn't like about him at all. Another was how he would always tell me about this one friend Seth from Florida, and, more specifically, how this Seth could barely fit into this yellow Speedo, because he was so big, but wore it anyway, every time at the beach.

T.J. would get this look in his eyes talking about this stuff. He had it right now. It was different from usual. His pupils got sharper, kind of flecked with silver. It was like he hadn't eaten in a while. This time it was especially disconcerting, because now he very lightly said to me—

"Look, I'll show you how to do it some time."

He could see me in the mirror, that I had nothing to say. That if I could, I'd take back everything.

"What?" I finally said, just to fill some kind of space.

"Kidding!" he said after a minute. He patted my head, which I wasn't loving right now. I watched it happen in the mirror. That way it didn't quite seem like me he was touching. *"Kidding!"* he said again. "Jesus, you never had any brothers. That's right," he said. "Don't worry. For crying out loud, don't worry! I'm only *kidding!*"

THREE

I'm telling Claudia yes, right there.

I was telling her that right there was where it felt right. She had never done this before, not quite like this. I was in my boxer shorts, on my bed. It was still my old bunk beds then. I was lying on my back, up on my elbows. Claudia had slid her hands all the way up my thighs, up under the boxers, was moving them now, sort of squeezing at that place where your legs become your hips. You know, on the insides, where there's that tendon. I liked the position I was in, in this almost embarrassing way. Because my legs were spread a little bit, and I was on my back. It was all vulnerable, like I was the girl or something. But don't get me wrong: I just liked how I was offering myself up to Claudia. You know, saying do whatever.

"So like this?" she was saying.

"Yeah," I said.

"What feels so much better about it?"

"I don't know," I said. "It just feels different. Like real warm. Like you're touching all of me. I don't know."

These conversations were standard issue when we were together like this. Like those times at Montgomery Mall, where we'd sneak into the Gap dressing room. This was before there were those pointless attendants all wired to some headphone system, the ones who show you to your room and then practically ask can they watch you change. This was when you could just go in, and if you were me and Claudia, spend an hour back there and no one would really notice. We'd be in the dressing room, down to our underwear, just pointing to parts of each other, certain areas, saying we liked them. She liked my arms. I liked the dimples in her hips, her thighs, her calves—I guess I was pretty much obsessed with everything when it came to Claudia, if you want to know the truth.

At first these moments had been kind of tense, because Claudia was Catholic, and dealing with two types of guilt: the standard-issue, hermetical guilt from the religion, and then the kind that comes from being young, transplanted to America, and therefore not really caring about worship or God in any real way anymore. But once she stopped wondering if touching me was about to get her showered in brimstone, we'd have these very open conversations. Like is this okay? Does this feel right? Do you like this better?

"Do you want me to do anything else?" Claudia was now asking.

"No," I said. "Just this. Just like that."

So she keeps on moving her hands right there, all the way up. I don't know how to describe how I felt. It was a new feeling, real mature—that one where you want the girl under your skin so bad you sort of consider cutting yourself. You know what I mean. Just so you'll feel more open.

So I lift up my shirt. It was a Smashing Pumpkins shirt, the one you had to wear after Kurt Cobain put that gun in his mouth like a jackass. I was doing this just so I could show Claudia what she was doing to me, and I started tugging on the elastic lining of my boxers, saying please take these off. Claudia was always the more rational one, which explains her saying—

"But your *mom* is right in there."

"It's fine," I said. "Oh it's fine."

"What are you talking about?"

"She's watching *Jeopardy!*," I explained. "She's like *obsessed*. Don't worry. She won't get up till it's over."

"What about T.J.?" she asked.

"I think he's in there with her. Don't worry. He knows not to come in."

"Are you sure?"

"Yeah."

"Wait," Claudia now said. "Do you tell T.J. about us?"

"No."

"Are you sure?" Claudia asked.

"Why would T.J. wanna come in right now?" is all I said.

So Claudia slides my boxers down to my knees. I felt more awkward than I thought I would, sort of propped up on my elbows, still in this T-shirt, my boxers now at my knees, my jeans at my ankles. You know, everything ready to be pulled up in case of an emergency. And, see, the lights were on, so I was very visible. It was like she was examining me.

"I kinda like looking at you," Claudia was saying. "Does it still feel good?"

"You don't even know."

"For real?"

"Yeah," I said. "Just like that. I mean, it feels different. It really feels different."

My eyes had pretty much been closed the whole time, but now, with this feeling burning even more, right in the middle of me, I opened them up and looked right at Claudia. I look right at her face, can see her moving, her shoulders moving, just barely. I feel my mouth opening now. Claudia's smiling. I see her eyes, I look right into them. Yeah, I'm really feeling it now, the first time ever. I close my eyes. Yeah. Just keep doing like that, right there. Yes. My stomach muscles cramp up, same with the tendons in my neck. Jesus. Yes. Yes. My mouth tingles, my lips and cheeks go sort of numb. Even my toes feel funny, dipped in ice—

Jesus. I'm very seriously now considering peeling my entire skin off and wrapping it around Claudia. Yes. Yes. Nothing in the world can be broken. I see that now. Yes. Throw glass plates against the wall and they'll just bounce off, glide down to the floor. Yes. Yes. Oh, God. Everything's so lucid, like it all belongs to me. Yes. Like even the colors are mine—

And right now I'd have yelled, but I knew there was no point to it. Oh God yes! I'm not scared of anything. I just knew that no sound would have come out—

"Oh . . . *God*," I suddenly hear Claudia saying. "Oh . . . *wow*."

I was taking in that one deep breath now, that horrible breath that comes all of a sudden, where you realize you don't really own anything. That nothing is yours. Then I opened my eyes and there was Claudia. She was so still, and still smiling. There was something confusing about looking at her. I can't explain it. A little time passed, and she said—

"Your forehead is so sweaty."

"I can feel it," I said. "I know."

"I'm going to go wash my hands now," she said.

"Yeah," I said. "Okay. That's fine."

FOUR

You wouldn't think it, because of the way he looked, all gentle and soft, and because he knew how to make origami flowers and fold napkins into swans, but T.J. was into wrestling. I discovered this pretty quick once he moved in. Whenever we were hanging out around the house, we'd get into these wrestling matches. They were fun for a while. He was tall, well over six feet, and I was still short for my age, something like five-six, so he could pick me up, throw me onto the couch, things like that. Or a lot of the time he'd just get me by the wrists, both of them, bend them back until I could feel it even in my elbows. That's what he was doing right now, about three hours after Claudia had left. Mom had just gone up to bed, and we were right there on the living room floor, in front of the turned-off television. He was pulling them, my wrists, like—

"Say mercy! Come on now, say it!"

"Never!"

"How about now?" He was twisting them even farther back.

"Never!" I said again. "Nope!"

"You don't have a chance!"

"Oow!"

"I told you."

"Fine," I said. "Mercy."

And he let go, but it's not like the match was over. But this time, as we got tangled back in each other, T.J. tried a new move. Up to this point his winning repertoire consisted pretty much of mercy, or that thing where you weave your arms up under someone's armpits, put your hands behind their neck, so they can't really move anymore. But what he was doing right now was different, and I didn't really get the point.

I mean, I didn't understand exactly what the point was of grabbing my ass like that.

So I squirmed away, quick.

"Oh, is someone scared?" T.J. said.

This was one of his favorite things to say when we wrestled, but right now it was registering different. I didn't want him to know this though, so I just said no, no one's scared, not me, and kept trying to pin him down. And here it comes again: his hand, up the back of my thigh. And look, it wasn't like I was eight years old. I could tell what was up, how T.J. was doing it in this way meant to seem like an accident. Like it was really my shoulder he was going for, but, oops, my ass ended up in his hand.

I knew something unorthodox was certainly taking place here. But then, at the same time, there was that one very true point that T.J. made continually: that I never had a brother, that he was just kidding, that if I had a brother I'd get it. I'd see how it was all just some sort of joke.

"Who's scared?" T.J. was still saying.

I wasn't doing such a brilliant job at pinning him down. He had me on my back now, my legs bent, my knees up at my mouth, like I was a gymnast or something. I was completely immobile, and wasn't having any fun anymore.

"Who's scared?" he said again.

"I'm not scared," I said. "I just can't move."

"Oh come on. You gotta at least try."

"I *am* trying."

"That's the best you can do? Come on now."

"Look I can't *move*."

"How about now?" he asked, but he was only coming down on me harder. And there was his damn hand again. I tried to squirm away again, but I couldn't move, not at all.

"I think somebody's scared," T.J. said, right in my ear. I felt the carpet against my cheek. I felt T.J.'s stubble against the other. It felt like coral.

"I don't think so," I said.

And really, it didn't bother me all that much. I wasn't some kid. Even right now, as his hand goes right up into my crotch for a second, and squeezes, and I hear him laughing a bit, and it's in this way like he can't even wait until he's alone. That's the kind of laugh it was, the kind you're not supposed to share with anyone. But I told you, I could just shut off my senses if I wanted to and that's what I did, went cold, dead, waiting eagerly until he grabbed my wrists again. Because then I could say mercy, and everything would be over.

"You okay?" T.J. was asking now.

"Of course," I said.

"You know I'm just kidding around with you?" he said.

"Yeah," I said. "Of course."

———

The only thing I was really sad about that night was that I no longer wanted to tell T.J. about what had happened earlier, with me and Claudia. I mean it's not that I didn't get it. I understood. I just wanted to tell him, because it made me feel older. But when T.J. asked about her, like he always did, all obsessive, in the bathroom now, I just said—

"She was too worried about you and Mom to really do anything."

I still tell so many stupid lies, and every time they just end up making everything worse. Like now, when T.J. said—

"Well, that's okay. Gives you something to think about in the bathroom."

God, was I pissed off. Not that I showed it. I never show people when I'm angry. I just told T.J. goodnight, said I was going to the kitchen, to get a glass of water. But really I just went in there and very quietly opened up the silverware drawer. We had these cheap steak knives, with the serrated blades, and I took one out. And look, it just made sense to push it down on my hand, on my knuckles like that. I still do this sometimes, and no one gets it. I have a stupid tendency to mention it to women, this habit, like they'll actually understand. But all they end up doing is just looking at me like they're deaf. It just makes me feel stupid. That's it. I'm not saying I'm some genius, but sometimes you just want to feel real dumb.

So I pressed down now—

I moved the blade just slightly over my knuckles. Then I put it back and looked at my hand. Here it comes. Yeah, there's the blood. It's right when you see the blood that you feel dumb.

But I'm in bed now, and still can't relax. So I call up Claudia. She says my voice sounds funny, but I just ignore her, and ask her for something, a favor. It was about the most hysterical request you've ever heard, so it made sense that her response was—

"Wait, what do you *mean*?"

"You know, just tell me how to do it. What you just did."

"Are you serious?"

"Are you in bed?"

"No, I'm sitting with my parents watching television."

"Serious?"

"No," she said. "Of course I'm in bed. It's eleven o'clock."

"So?" I said. "Will you?"

It wasn't like phone sex. I want to be clear about this. What happened was more like phone instructions, like one of those lines you can call about cooking a turkey right, or programming the VCR. Only this was how to get yourself off. I didn't want Claudia to tell me to close my eyes, and pretend she was right there in some freak lingerie she'd never wear in real life. It was nothing like that. I just wanted her to tell me how to do it, alone, by myself. If that makes any sense.

It was funny. My knuckles hadn't had time to scab over, and the movement of my hand was making them bleed a lot more than you'd think. Other than that, I don't think the details are worth going into. I mean, they're so easy to conjure up on your own, commonplace enough.

"Did you do it yet?" Claudia asked at one point. It was taking some time, but she was so patient.

"No, not yet," I said.

"I don't really know what to say anymore."

"Just tell me what to do," I said.

And what can you really say about it once it did finally happen? That it was climactic? Because that's not really what seems important.

What's so perfect is the conversation me and Claudia had afterward. I thanked her a lot, and she was all like you're welcome, you're welcome.

Then she told me about herself. This was the really crazy part.

"Hey you know what?" she said.

"Huh?"

"I do it too," she said.

"What's that?"

"What you just did," she said. "I do it too. In my own way I mean. I've sort of been doing it forever."

"No way," is all I could say to this.

"I did it just now," she said.

"What?"

"I just did it," she said. "The same thing you did."

"No way!" I said.

"That's why I kept asking if you were finished," she said. "I was already done. I was being selfish."

"You bitch!"

"Whatever."

"I didn't know girls did it."

"They do," she said. "At least I do."

"Well," I said.

"I know."

"That's crazy,"

"Oh *shit*," Claudia said. "My mom's about to yell at me for being on the phone."

"I just can't believe it."

"Meet me by my locker in the morning," Claudia said. "I gotta go."

I just laid there for a minute now, very still, looking up at the ceiling like it may open up, lift me straight up to God knows where. But then the phone, one of those *Sports Illustrated* football kind, started making that annoying chopping sound. I hung it up, then decided I'd do it again, what the hell, completely by myself now. It was fine—well, almost. I mean the blood had dried up finally. The only problem was that right there, of all the things I could think about, I end up thinking about T.J. Right afterward, I mean. I thought about how he was right. It pissed me off how he was so right about everything. About how now everybody was doing it.

FIVE

I've learned since not to talk about sex, not with anybody. Bring the subject up with me today and I'll just sit there, look at you until you shut up. I won't even ask the simplest questions. If you're lucky I'll nod. That's it.

But it was different then, different that next night. I was in the bathroom with T.J. and I just sort of wanted him to know I was thinking about it, seriously considering having sex. The thing was, I wasn't. I just wanted him to *think* I was, because that way I'd be older to him, more like a friend. You know, less like a brother.

"How old were you?" I was asking him.

"Fifteen," he said. "I was fifteen."

"Do you think fourteen's too young?"

"I don't know. Maybe. No."

"It's not like I *feel* fourteen with her," I said.

"Watch out," T.J. said, putting his hand on my shoulder, leaning forward to wet his face in the sink. He used very hot water, part of his strict hygiene routine. I always had to add the cold, and wait, when I washed my face.

"What about, you know, condoms?" I asked.

"What about them?"

"I don't know. They seem annoying."

"They are," T.J. said.

He was sort of laughing, by the way.

"Yeah," I said.

"Have you ever tried to put one on?"

"What do you mean?" I asked.

"What do you mean, what do I mean?" T.J. said. "Have you ever tried to put a condom on, when you're alone?"

I wasn't sure what to say here. I mean, of course I had tried to put a condom on when I was alone. When you're fourteen, and have erections ninety percent of the time, you come up with ways to pass the time. So of course one day I had gone down the street to the 7-Eleven, like I just wanted a Big Gulp, and stole a box of Trojans. And I nearly went through all of them trying to get one on. But I didn't think it was necessary to go into all that, so I just said, real adultlike—

"Yeah."

"Yeah what?" T.J. said.

"Yeah I maybe have put one on before."

"Okay, now we're getting somewhere," he said. "Watch out."

He was leaning into the sink, spitting his toothpaste out.

"Yeah," I said, "and they are sort of annoying."

I turned the water to cooler now, wet my face. I had never really been too into washing my face before T.J. started living with us, but he was always stressing how important it was to be clean. So I squeezed the soap into my hand, Oil of Olay we used, and started scrubbing. T.J. was talking about condoms still.

"Can I ask you something?" he was saying.

I nodded, bent down, turned on the water, and was rinsing my face when T.J. asked pretty much the most personal question anyone's ever asked me.

"Were you hard or soft when you put it on?"

I just kept throwing water onto my face, like I was the dirtiest kid ever, had spent all day smearing mud and grease all over my face, and was trying to get the last of it. But eventually I had to stand back up and look at T.J. in the mirror. I didn't say anything. I just looked at him.

"So?" he said.

"What's that?" I finally said.

"Hard or soft?"

"Oh . . . ," I said.

"Hey, if you can't have this conversation, what are you gonna do when it comes to actually having sex?"

That had been the problem with T.J. He always had these sterling points on tap that made me feel like an idiot. But the thing was, I hadn't been all that nervous, or uncomfortable with the topic, considering the almost clinical way that me and Claudia spoke to each other. Not to mention this was the mid-nineties, when AIDS education was all the rage. From fifth grade on my teachers had found every way possible to tell us about AIDS, about herpes— hell, they'd find ways to sneak syphilis into a trig equation. Still, I couldn't for the life of me remember anyone talking about condoms being used except when you were anything *but* hard. Like what were all those awkward banana analogies for anyway?

So I spoke up—

"Hard," I said.

"That's the thing," T.J. said. He was all calm, like we were talking about a baseball player, how his stats didn't show how vital he was to the team. "That's just the thing."

"What is?"

"Being hard," he said. "It's more difficult," he said. "Putting them on, when you're hard."

"It's harder when you're hard?" I asked. To this day, that may be the stupidest thing that's ever come out of my mouth. But T.J. didn't seem to think it was funny at all. In fact, he was getting more serious.

"Exactly," he said.

"Really?"

"Yes," he said. "A lot of people don't know this. When they're young I mean. Like you."

"Oh," I said.

"Yeah. You know that kind of halfway state? That's what you're after. That's what you want. Do you know what I mean?"

"I think so."

"And then you put it on and it's easier. Then you get yourself hard, *into* the condom," he said.

This was a lot to digest. I'll be honest. For the most part, I thought he was full of shit, even more confused than me. But then again, if you'd have seen this guy, how handsome he was, you'd just know this guy had been with plenty of women. I mean, he hadn't dated anyone yet in Maryland, but he had lived in Florida of all places. I figured Florida was a much more sexual place than Maryland. So as I placed my toothbrush under the tap, put the toothpaste on it, and started brushing, I thought about all this. Taking into account the adventure I'd had trying to get a condom on, it started to seem like maybe there was some sense to what T.J. was saying. Maybe he could see this, my thought process, see it on my face, because I was spitting in the sink when I heard him saying—

"Do you have any condoms left? Look, I'll show you what I mean."

I put some water in my mouth, sloshed it around. Then I spit it out. I stood up straight. I didn't say anything.

"Do you have any condoms?"

And still I didn't say anything, but it was the strangest thing: I was nodding. I was saying yes.

"Where?" he asked.

Not saying anything, I opened the drawer under the sink. Before I could even get a condom out, T.J. was squatting down at my knees, digging in there, fishing one out.

"Okay," he was now saying, tearing it open, holding the

thing in his hand now. "You know you put this end down, right? You sort of pinch the top like this."

I was watching it all in the mirror, even though he was right next to me. But now, as he slid his boxers down, the sink was blocking him in the mirror. You know what I mean. So I sort of glanced down to my left, at him next to me. And I'll admit that it was comforting for a minute, at first, to see that I was pretty much the same size, because it's not like me and my friends were so mature that we hung out all day with our boxers around our knees.

But then I just got that empty feeling that I think everyone gets looking at men like this. Or maybe it's just me. But I'm convinced there's just something sad and empty to looking at men in this state. They look helpless.

"All right," T.J. was saying. "Are you even watching here?"

"Yeah," I said.

"Do you see what I mean?" he said. "Look. See what I mean?"

I just nodded. He didn't really seem like he was all that interested in my responses anymore.

"Just like this," he was saying. "That kind of halfway state. Yup, just like this."

But here's the thing: I wasn't trying to watch all that intently. Like the wrestling, I was just waiting for this moment in my life to be over because you knew the next one, whatever came right after this, would be better. But I could see enough to grasp that he was having even more trouble than I'd had. I mean, that thing wasn't getting on him anytime soon.

"Yup," he was still saying. "Sort of just like this. Damn it. Wait. Here, here," he said. "Just like this. You just roll it right over. See?"

Again I nodded. This time, just sort of at myself, in the mirror. Like yes, this really is your life. I mean, it's one thing when a guy looks helpless, but T.J. was now far beyond that infamous halfway state.

"Okay!" he was now saying. "Okay! Look at that. Here we go. See there? Told you, didn't I tell you? Are you even watching this?"

I nodded. But maybe my eyes were closed.

"Yeah, yeah. Now feel that."

"What?"

"So you know. Give me your hand. Come on. Quick. You should feel this, so you know," he said.

"I don't know—"

"Yeah, yeah!" he was saying. "Seriously! Come here!" he said. "Come here! Quick! Oh, God! Feel that right there!"

———

So all that really happened next is I slipped up a bit. It was like this: I was downstairs having lunch with Mom, and she was telling some joke about T.J. with one of her employees, something about how T.J. was stuck in the closet or whatever. He wasn't living with us anymore, turned out he had no design skills and Mom had to fire him. He was back in Florida now, waiting on John Ritter at the Ritz Carlton Hotel.

"He's *so* stuck in the closet," Mom's employee was saying.

"*Totally,*" Mom said. They were laughing pretty hard.

"Oh I know what you mean," I said.

It's funny, how this just came out. I was laughing myself, or at least trying to, but all of a sudden the two of them were looking at me all serious, like I had done something wrong.

"Wait," Mom was now saying. "What do you mean exactly?"

But it wasn't with her I went into all the detail. That was with the damn detective she hired. You just should have seen that guy. You should have heard the questions he asked me, the way he wanted to know every last part of the story. He kept saying I'm sorry, I really am, but could you please be more specific? Like when you say he didn't touch you anywhere, where *exactly* didn't he touch you? No, he didn't touch me. Not really. I don't think. No one ever touched me. Do you understand? Listen to me, please. Listen to me—

But he wasn't listening. This was his job. This is how he paid for his house, how he fed his kids, how he bought his wife new curtains. And I was messing this up. That's why he always seemed so mad at me for holding back.

PART TWO

CHILDREN AT PLAY

Perhaps he expected to be punished upon his return, for what, what crime exactly, he did not expect to know, since he had already learned that, though children can accept adults as adults, adults can never accept children as anything but adults too.

—William Faulkner, *Light in August*

SIDE MIRRORS ARE POINTLESS

Slow down! Cousin Stacey was all like slow down! *Please!*
She was really flipping out, in that annoying teenage-girl
way, real exaggerated, like if they don't have something to
panic about they'll actually go crazy.

I was hearing her, but I wasn't really listening. We were
in my Honda Prelude, driving all sorts of reckless around
Uncle Ray's new neighborhood. He had moved out of that
little awful home, in that neighborhood no one really knew
about, and into this neighborhood that didn't even exist the

year before. It was one of these developments of wannabe plastic mansions, everything so new there wasn't even grass yet. No front lawns. No backyards. Just dirt, a ton of dirt, dirt with bulldozer tracks on it. And these huge houses, all done up in this shade of brown I can only describe as very tame. Most of them were still up for sale, the houses. That's the type of neighborhood this was, where no matter what, most of the houses would be up for sale. And there were three models total, every third one you passed was the same. So driving around, it was impossible to feel like you were going anywhere. It was like driving on a treadmill.

But right now I was just really liking the roads back here. You should have seen these roads. They were so new, that smooth muted black, not one crack anywhere. It was like me and Stacey were the first ones driving on these roads ever, and you just had to go fast. She was eighteen now, me fifteen. I was on my learner's permit, so I needed her in the car, to be legal. But I was still the one teaching her how to drive stick.

"Oh God come on slow *down*," she was saying. "You're gonna *kill* us."

"What are you talking about?" I said. "Just re*lax*."

"I'll relax when you slow down."

It was stunning. There really was no one back here. Every time I came with Dad to Ray's there was this part of me that was convinced he was the only one who lived back here. I had never been in the car with anyone but Mom, so this was the first time I didn't have to drive according to ten thousand rules. I was hitting fifty now, in fourth gear, going in and out of these little pools of yellow light from the streetlamps. Everything so new, the light hit the ground in the most perfect circles. There wasn't even one bug or moth caught up in the bulbs yet.

"See, just watch this," I was saying. "My foot's going onto the clutch, and I'm shifting down, to go faster."

"I can't pay attention with you like this."

"Relax," I said. "We're not going that fast anymore. Just watch. I'm shifting down, and now you'll see, we'll pick up a ton of speed."

"*Jesus!*" Stacey said.

"I know, right?"

"Okay," she said. "Now at least stop for a second."

"Fine," I said. "Okay."

I stopped right in the middle of the road. I put it in neutral, tugged the emergency brake. I couldn't get over it. I mean, you could just do stuff like that back here.

————

What happened is this: the year before, during my freshman year, just after all that fun went down with T.J., Dad tells me he's leaving. He was moving out of Maryland. The best part is that Dad had met this woman through one of those dating services, not the want ads for love in the newspaper, but those ridiculous clubs that everyone was joining around this time, when suddenly there were no more married people and adults didn't know what to do with themselves. Her name's Mary, of all things. I think Dad has some fetish for foreigners, probably from growing up in a part of Maine where you often ended up dating distant relatives, because Mary's Filipino. She's crazy, too.

So Dad met her through this pathetic organization, on some ski trip. And Dad doesn't even ski. But that's how he met her, skiing. And after about ten minutes of deep reflection, he reaches the epiphany that he should move into her house, in this hick part of New Jersey with, I believe, one of this country's highest densities of rat tails and cross-eyed people.

And look, I got the point by now. Dad was feeling pretty low. Since Jiffy's shut down after that murder out back, he'd been working a string of ridiculous jobs, most recently at Kentucky Fried Chicken. Dad was at a point in his life where he was forty years old and would end up talking to you for an hour about rotisserie chickens and not even know it. And this Mary was a nurse. Dad was hoping some of it would rub off on him, I guess. I mean the guy had been temporarily living with his brother for nearly a decade.

But this wasn't how Dad put it when he sat me down

one day, when we were at this bar, that same bar from when I was a kid actually, a martini in front of him, a beer for me this time around. There we are when Dad very formally says—

"Hey there, feller, somethin' I gotta talk to you about."

"What's up?"

"You know Mary?" he asked.

"Who's Mary?" I knew who she was, but I had developed this smart-ass way of speaking.

"You know, the woman I've been seein'."

"Oh, right," I said. "The skier?"

"The nurse," Dad said.

"Dad, I'm kidding. Chill. I know who Mary is." I had never met her before, though.

"Well," he said. "I'm gonna be movin' in with her. Livin' together."

"No shit? Where does she live again?"

"Up in New Jersey."

"Wow," I said. "I didn't realize things were so . . . I mean, *wow*."

"Yeah," he said. "Don't I know it."

"Do you even *know* her?" I asked.

But Dad sort of ignored this, went on to babble about how it's really nothing, a four-hour drive that he'd do once a month. It was funny, the way I felt, sitting there, watching the bubbles in my beer shooting up and shattering against the surface, the bartender topping off Dad's martini. I mean, I just didn't care. I didn't care about him leaving, but it was in the sense that if he walked outside and a bus happened to drive right into him and his organs ended up smeared all over the windshield and they ended up having to use the wipers to get them off—well, I wouldn't really care about that either. I'd thought about a lot of things in terms like that back then. I still do.

What's really funny is when I get home that day the first thing I do is go straight to the fridge. And I take out the carton of eggs, open it up, just look at the eggs for a long time. I just stare at the things, these soft white ovals. I've always liked how eggs always have shadows on them, no matter the light. Then I pick one up, hold it above the sink, and break it in my fist. Then I take another, throw it into the sink, hard enough that the yoke flies up and gets me in the face. And then, you should have seen it. I'm taking all these eggs, and just throwing them, against the cabinets, into the walls, on the floor. I'm going crazy with these eggs. It was tremendous. There just weren't enough of them. That's the problem with throwing eggs into walls. There's never enough.

———

For about a year Dad's pretty true to his word. He drove down from Jersey about once a month, for a weekend, always alone, not once with Mary or her kid—I forgot to mention this little seven-year-old girl she had, Melanie. I'm sorry. I just always forget these people really exist. Anyway, she's from Mary's first marriage to some guy who Dad always referred to as a real lunatic.

Today, a Saturday, Dad had arrived in the morning, pulled up into Mom's driveway in this absurd car I'm going to tell you about in a minute. We hung out all day, shot some pool, hit up the standard bar for Dad's prenightcap, and ended up at Ray's for dinner.

Cousin Mike wasn't around because he had entered this new phase in life where if he wasn't getting stoned or at least lighting something on fire, or getting in a fight, or getting a tattoo of a pot leaf on his bicep, he was at his mother's house, at Aunt Edie's, up in his room staring at a wall. And now he's in the army. But I already told you that—

But Stacey was there, and that I liked, because I hadn't seen her in forever. Dad had this weird friend Donnie come over too, some guy who I guess Dad had known for a long time but who I certainly had never seen. I've noticed that divorced parents often have these types of acquaintances: people who just seem to show up, but were really there the whole time. I mean, remember Floyd? You haven't already forgotten about Floyd, have you? Like really, who the hell was Floyd?

He was a freak, this Donnie, and both me and Stacey

could just tell, just by the way he ate and how he insisted on using one of those curly children's straws with his red wine. It was purple, that straw, and it gave you the creeps, which is why the minute dinner was over, me and Stacey told everyone we were going out for a bit, to drive around in my Honda.

———

"Okay," I was saying to Stacey now. We were still stopped, still right in the middle of the road. I don't think these roads even had names yet. "Put your hand over mine and you'll see."

"You'll go slower this time?"

"Will you chill?"

"Promise me you'll go slower."

"All right, all right."

So Stacey puts her hand over mine. The past few years had been rough for her. Since her parents divorced later, she had to deal with thinking all the time about which one she was supposed to love and which one she was supposed to hate—stuff I had been lucky enough to avoid. I think that's part of why she kept dropping out of high school, because she was sort of a wreck and no one was listening. She kept getting moved into different ones, so even though she was eighteen she was only one grade above me. Point being, it didn't feel like we were that far apart in age anymore. Besides, I've always got on well with older people. Most of the time when people meet me they think I'm at least five years older than I really am. I'll probably look a hundred when I'm only fifty. After all, I didn't even have a license and I was still the one teaching her how to drive here.

"Okay," I was saying. "See my foot? I'm down on the clutch, and putting it into first. This is the tricky part. If I lift up too quick, we'll stall, like this—"

"*Jesus!*" Stacey said. "Isn't that bad for the car?"

"Only if you do it like every five minutes," I said. "Don't worry."

I did it again, without stalling, going slow and easy, not so much for Stacey's comfort, but so she could see how to do it right. That way I felt even more adult, and professional, two qualities that had started to become important to me. I don't know why.

I put it in second now, then third, and we just coasted around. Stacey kept her hand on mine. I liked it. I like that stuff, how with family you can not see someone for years and then out of nowhere they'll put their hand on you and it's fine.

This was especially nice because around this time something had started happening that I wasn't too fond of. I guess it started up just after all the fun went down with T.J., but I feel like blaming him is sort of cheating. Anyway, something was happening, and I wasn't liking it. With girls,

I mean. I had broke up with Claudia the year before, just started treating her like I hated her until she decided not to talk to me anymore, like it was a mission or something that I had no control over. And ever since then if any girl touched me I'd get real uneasy. Sometimes I still get it, a lot actually. A girl will touch me, on the back of my neck or wherever, and I just want them to get off. It's like they're accusing me of something.

————

But I'm leaving things out, things I said I'd mention. When Dad got into town earlier that day he had a surprise. He had bought me this car. And not just any car, but a Mercedes.

Dad had picked up this 1970 rust-gold Mercedes sedan from a New Jersey junkyard. I don't know. I guess it's a popular thing to do in that part of Jersey, buying stuff from junkyards and calling it new. So he bought it, fixed the engine, because Dad was always into fixing things. I swear, if he had rich parents he'd have been a doctor, probably a damn good one too.

But this Mercedes was something. The only piece of the interior left was the driver's seat, which I'll admit was in stellar condition, hardly a crack in the leather. But still, that didn't take away the fact that Dad had to use a lawn chair for the passenger's seat, and a mattress cut in half for the back.

"Pretty nice, huh?" Dad said when he got out in Mom's driveway. "Got me all the way here without a problem."

"That's some car," I said. "It really is."

These kind of moments started to occur a lot back then, and I never knew what I was supposed to say when they happened. I could just so clearly see that I was on my way to becoming Mom's kid completely. I was fine with this, because Mom's certainly a better example of pretty much everything than Dad, but I still felt bad for him. You could just feel him losing his own kid, even I could feel it, and I *was* the kid. You felt it all up in your bones, behind your eyes even. And you thought: what's an adult worth once something like that happens, once he doesn't know his own kid anymore?

"Sure is," Dad was saying. "And I'll tell you somethin'. The amazing thing is that it's got climate control—that still *works*."

Dad can't get enough of things like this. A car can clearly be an old piece of junk, but say something obscure like the climate control is still functioning, that's when Dad gets all obsessed. He won't even notice the rest of the car. He'll lay down under the thing, stuff enough rubber bands and whatever else up in the engine, just so it'll move and he'll have an excuse to use the vintage climate control. Told you he should have been a doctor. All they do is make a living jumpstarting people who should be dead.

"I can't believe it," I said. "Climate control."

"To the exact temperature you want," he said.

"To the degree," I said.

"Want it?" he said.

"What's that?"

"Want it? This car?" Dad said. "It's yours."

What's sad about this, though, was it was like he wasn't even seeing the Honda Prelude he was parked right next to.

"Dad that's something," I said. "But, see, Mom got me this car, this Honda right here."

"This Honda's yours?" he asked. "This Honda right here?"

I nodded.

"Jesus Christ, that's a nice car. Mom's doin' well, huh?"

"Yeah," I said. "She really is."

"The business really took off?"

"I guess it did."

Her little company really was something to brag about—there were four employees in our basement now—but it was funny: I didn't want to talk to Dad about Mom. I almost felt sort of protective of her, like if I told him about her life, and about the life I had with her, he'd find some way to take credit, at least in his head. Luckily, Dad was already changing the subject.

"I used to have a Honda," he was saying. "You remember that? A little blue Civic?"

"Of course," I said. "There was always candy on the floor."

"You remember the candy?" he said.

"Caramel Creams," I said. "I'll always remember this time when you were supposed to pick me and Mom up from the airport, but—"

"Well, this is somethin'," Dad was saying. He wasn't really paying attention to me anymore. I was okay with this. "This is a hell of car, isn't it?"

I just nodded. Then we just stood in the driveway for a moment, just loitering. And Dad was obviously still caught up in this moment, with my Honda Prelude, because right now, as me and Stacey came back into the house, Dad was still talking about it, with Ray and this Donnie guy. And he wasn't just talking about it the way normal people talk about things.

Me and Stacey park the car in the driveway, come in through the front door, turn the corner into the dining room, and you should have seen it.

There's Dad, standing on the dining room table, Ray and Donnie around him laughing like sea lions, saying—

"A goddamn Honda! This sporty little Honda!"

"A *Honda*!" Donnie yelled.

"Exactly!" Dad said. He started jumping up and down on the table.

"No jumping on the table," Ray said.

"A Honda!" Donnie yelled again, like making sure he understood.

"These are our parents," Stacey said to me. "Do you realize that?"

"That's my Dad on your dad's table," I said.

"Hondas are junk anyway," Ray was saying.

Ever since Ray moved into this big house, and started making some real money, he had constantly been trying to adopt a classier lifestyle. For him this just meant calling Hondas junk and eating brie cheese all the time. Like say you were over, he'd throw a thing of brie at you, and these little bright white wafer crackers. He said the crackers were the most expensive crackers in the cheap-cracker aisle. That's a typical Ray joke. And if he was trying to be extra sophisticated, he'd heat up the cheese a bit, like the French do, but in a microwave. It did taste pretty good warm, I have to say.

It could also make a pretty fantastic mess if you were Dad and happened to be standing on a table and laughing to death and yelling about a Honda and didn't even realize you just stepped right into the cheese.

"Oh *shit!*" Dad said.

"We've got an emergency," Donnie said. "Cheese down, cheese down."

"Shit!"

"No worries, no worries," Ray said.

"The cheese is down."

Dad was getting off the table now. He took his sock off, just placed it in the pile of brie. The sock was brown, with little maroon diamonds stitched on it.

"No worries," Ray said again. "The whole fridge is filled with brie."

Me and Stacey didn't see what was so funny about this comment. In fact, we figured things had maybe settled down to the point where we could announce our presence in the room. So we walked over and sat down with the three of them. But they didn't even notice us.

That's how hard they were laughing at what Ray had said.

"A whole fridge of brie!" Donnie was saying.

"I know!" Ray said.

"My sock's in the cheese," Dad pointed out.

Stacey looked at me and smiled. I smiled back. Then she reached over for the wine and took a sip, straight from the bottle. It wasn't a normal bottle either, but one of those jugs, I don't know what they're called, with the funny little circular handles. She took another sip, passed it to me. Dad and them were still laughing, but it was like the second we picked up the bottle some radar went off in all of them. They sensed something was wrong, missing, which is why Ray was suddenly saying—

"When the hell did you get back?"

"We've been sitting here with you guys the whole time," Stacey said. "We never went out, decided not to."

"It's true," I said.

"Car still working?" Dad asked.

"The Honda!" Donnie said.

"Don't get all smart with me," Ray was saying to Stacey.

Avoiding conflict with types like Ray and Dad is about the world's easiest thing: you just refill their glasses, like Stacey was doing right now for Ray. They were drinking out of plastic cups, the classy clear kind. There was a stack in the middle of the table, and after topping off Dad's glass, and this Donnie character's, Stacey grabbed two and filled them for me and her.

———

So we just sat around now, drinking the wine, talking about whatever. I guess it was more like they kept talking and me and Stacey listened and then looked at each other and sort of grinned. Like yes, no matter what, these people made us.

After a while the phone rings, and Stacey gets up and answers it. Since I was fifteen, I was extremely interested in other people's phone conversations, especially people around my age. I was always slightly convinced they had something to do with me. Stacey had that girl smile all over her face that's so obvious.

She was saying—

"*Now?* Are you sure? Right *now?*"

—very quietly, in this whisper so her dad couldn't hear. But it wasn't like she really seemed to care about anything when it came to Ray, because when she got off the phone the first thing out of her mouth was—

"I've gotta go."

Ray didn't even answer. There was a split second of quiet, then he went on talking about whatever he was talking about. I don't know what it was because I was just sitting there zoning out. I do that a lot, kind of forget I'm supposed to be actively participating in what's going on. What's even worse is sometimes I *feel* like I'm just zoning out, sitting there practically dead, but then it turns out I've been talking the whole time. If you want to know the truth, I tend to make myself the center of whatever's happening.

"It was fun," Stacey was saying to me now. She grabbed her glass, drank the rest in one sip. Then she put her hand on my head. "See you in ten years or something."

"Yeah," I said. "Thanks."

I haven't seen her since. I wouldn't mind knowing how she's doing. I just don't know who to ask.

"She's a good girl," Dad said a little later, after Stacey had gone upstairs, changed into a tighter pair of jeans, ran out the front door. It was right when the door shut that Dad spoke. "You've got a good girl, Ray," he said again.

"She's a fucking slut," Ray said.

Dad didn't say anything. He looked at me carefully, with this face to let me know two things: one, he didn't agree with Ray on this point, and two, he was too much of a coward to say anything about this out loud. I know I should have at least said something, but I didn't. So the only person left to talk was Donnie, who took a sip of his wine with that stupid straw, and then said—

"Anyone ever hear the one about the Honda?"

———

This new house of Ray's smelled of paint-thinner. He hadn't lived there long enough for it to have that family smell, different everywhere, but always very clearly the smell of people related to each other. I mean, this place was antiseptic. And it was so clearly a shoddy job, the construction. The banister wobbled when you went up the stairs. Most of the doorknobs practically came out in your hand. And I guess the wood floors were real, but they looked more like they'd been rolled out, then glued down. You were supposed to be so into the *idea* of this place, that you didn't notice you just moved into a piece of shit.

But it's so quiet right now, the four of us at the table. I told you about how my senses would suddenly just shut down, focus real hard on one thing. Well, that's what it's like right now. Close your eyes and you can hear all this in the house, all these mistakes. It's all you can hear. Come on, listen: like if a real serious storm came—the place would disintegrate, and we'd be sitting at this table, right here in these chairs, drinking this wine, in a pile of dirt looking out at the smoothest roads and driveways in the world.

And that turpentine, paint-thinner smell. God, it was getting so strong now. I swear my eyes were even watering up. Like I was actually crying, when Ray said—

"Oh God it's late."

"Jesus, it's one o'clock," Dad said.

"It's that time."

"It was that time three hours ago," Donnie said.

"Hey, feller," Dad said to me, "speakin' of that Honda, how's about I borrow the keys, to give Donnie a ride home."

"Maybe I can drive," I said.

"Oh I'll drive," Dad said.

"I think I better drive."

"Haven't you been drinking?" Dad asked.

"I only had one glass of wine. I'm fine."

"Sure?"

"There's no brie on any of my socks," I said.

"Well, I'm going to bed," Ray said. " 'Night."

And then he just up and left. That was it. I haven't seen him since. I don't really care what he's up to either.

"So you want to drive Donnie, just the *two* of you?" Dad asked.

"I can't do that," I said.

"Oh you know where he lives, it's just up around—"

"No," I said. "I just can't."

"Well why not?"

"See, with my learner's permit, I need you in the car," I said. "I can't drive without an adult."

———

The backseat of the Prelude was tiny, like designed only for the asses of hyperactive teenage girls. But since Donnie was pretty drunk it didn't seem to bother him, even though he was fat as hell. He just laid down, took up the whole thing. And the whole time he kept shouting—

"We're in the Honda! We're in the Honda!"

And each time it would only impress Dad even more.

"I know, I know!" he'd yell. "Can you believe it?"

"The infamous Honda!"

"Ray seemed like he was in a bad mood," I said at one point.

"The infamous!" Dad said.

I didn't say anything else really, during the drive to Donnie's, because he and Dad were so engaged in each other, all revved up. And on the way back I had a few things I felt like bringing up but I didn't say anything because Dad was asleep at that point. But the thing I want to tell you is when I actually got my license, a few months later, there was this time where I was driving down my street, Nelson Street, really late and I just started thinking about this night, sort of thinking about Dad in general. And before I know it I'm going eighty miles an hour, running all the stoplights, straight past my own home, just oblivious. And suddenly I'm slamming on the brakes, turning sharp to avoid this parked car that somehow got right in front of me. I drive straight into a tree. Every window breaks. The hood flies up and shatters the windshield. The side mirror clips some branch, flies into my window, shatters it. Glass got in my mouth, small pieces I could only feel. This girl I was trying to feel attracted to at the time was next to me. I had forgot all about her. Then I heard her screaming, all panicked. You know, the way girls get. But don't worry. She was fine.

FAMILY TRIP

I probably wasn't even two years old when the photo was taken, but that didn't seem to be comforting Mary at all. The second she saw it, she got all sorts of hostile.

"Joe, what is this?" she was saying. She was looking at the photo. She was Filipino, so even though she spoke English perfect, it always came out too fast. Everything she said sounded defensive.

"What's that, dear?" Dad asked.

"This," Mary said. "What is this? What is this?"

"Gimme a minute," Dad said. He wasn't in the room with the rest of us yet.

"This," Mary was saying. She was starting to lose it. I swear to you, Mary was always starting to lose it. "Joe," she was saying. "This, this, *this!*"

Dad comes into the room now. We were at his sister's house in Massachusetts, Aunt June's, were up for Easter, had just arrived after a long drive. I hadn't seen any of my family on Dad's side for about three years, since high school started and Dad moved away. So when he called up and asked do you want to come up, I said sure. We were sitting in the guest room now, with the queen-size bed for Dad and Mary, me sitting right there on the bed with Mary's kid, Melanie.

I'd like to tell you that I was thrilled to see my family on Dad's side, I really would, considering I hadn't seen them in years. But I'd be lying. With Dad not around anymore, I'd started liking him less, sort of forgot what he looked like sometimes, saw his background as something smart to avoid. I got into being a part of Mom's family, who were all these very smart types, doing like ten crossword puzzles a day, working real jobs, all that. I mean, no one on Dad's side ever went to college, don't think they really knew what it was, and here I was, talking after school to a guidance counselor about how if I get my grades up a little there's a chance I could find myself at a decent college.

Mostly I was just psyched to drive from Maryland to Dad's hick home in Jersey on my own. I wasn't curious to see where he'd been living all these years. I was seventeen now, had been stuck driving for a year in Rockville, where you'd hit a red light every three minutes, where you were never really going anywhere. See, Mom had been making money, and bought me this used Honda Prelude, but I didn't have it anymore. I totaled it the year before, like ten minutes after I turned sixteen, because this girl I didn't even like was annoying the hell out of me and I ended up in a tree. Now I had this twenty-year-old BMW, super hip, this black 528, plenty of chrome, red leather seats. We picked it up because it was cheap, supposedly couldn't go all that fast. But on the Jersey Turnpike I swear I got the thing up to ninety without any trouble.

Dad had pretty much stopped coming down to Maryland completely at this point. I was fine with this. I mean, he had this whole life up in Jersey now, with this woman, this little girl, and I was pretty okay with the idea of not knowing him anymore. He was actually going to some sort of college even, one of these specialty get-ups for middle-age people, to learn how to be one of those people who take blood before you see the real doctor. A vascular technician. It was one of those jobs that Sally Struthers never used to be quiet about on television. Remember them? Like gun repair.

On top of this, Dad was working the graveyard shift at

a place called the Ding Dong Deli. So he was busy as hell, I understood. He'd call up every now and then, I guess like twice a year at this point, always when family stuff came up. You should have been on the line during one of these chats. The beginnings were always so awkward. Neither of us knew how to say even normal things. We didn't know how to say hello right, couldn't figure out how to ask how are you. Eventually, this settled, and Dad would bring up some family gathering, ask if I had any interest. This Easter was the first time T.J. wasn't going to be around. He was staying in Florida this year. That's why I went. It turned out he'd actually been arrested. He went to jail, and it was still against the law for me to see him.

———

"Hey Mom, what is it?" Melanie was now asking. She was around nine, I think.

"Joe, what is this?" Mary was still saying. She was talking so loud still. It was like she didn't know Dad was right there. And he was even touching her.

"I think I'm missing somethin'," Dad said. "What's going on?"

"This photo is what I mean," Mary said.

"Mom," Melanie said. Everything she said sounded sad and whiny. She had these glossy buck teeth that made it hard for her to speak like a normal person. Every syllable involved a lot of saliva. On the outside of her mouth, I mean. "Mom," she said again. "What's the matter, mom? Are you *crying*?"

———

Like I said, I wasn't even two when the photo had been taken. I looked over at it and I couldn't remember that day, or even that time. It was one of those cheesy professional portraits, Olan Mills or whatever. The background was a bunch of fake trees, not plastic and three dimensional, just like a big poster smeared with fake trees. It was supposed to be all pretty and tranquil, the beginnings of the most spectacular fall in the history of the seasons. There was fake sunlight. The leaves on the fake trees were orange, red, brown, yellow—

"Oh relax," Dad was saying now. "Just relax. Please."

—and then, in the foreground, was Dad and Mom. They were just standing there.

"Please," he was saying. "Let's just calm down here."

You should have seen how funny the two of them looked. They were smiling. Dad looked so young. He was around twenty-three I guess, very thin. Mom was a little older. She looks exactly the same today, because Mom's the type of woman who spends the first half of her life looking older than everyone else and then the second half looking ten times younger.

"Come on honey," Dad said.

They were looking straight out, sort of vapid and forced. And in between them, all wrapped up in this white blanket, was a little baby. It had the kind of relaxed look babies get. Like stare at them forever, and as long as they keep that look you'll never know if they're about to start laughing or crying. I can still pull off that look, at least for a little bit. Then I start laughing. I'm pretty much always laughing, just so you know.

And I know that baby was me. But I mean it was so long ago that I couldn't remember any of it and didn't care about it at all, which is a lot more than I can say for Mary.

She was actually crying.

"It's no big deal," Dad was saying. He had his arm around Mary. She was shaking. You could see this more because of how Dad's arm was moving, in these erratic up-and-down jolts. I was sitting on the bed with Melanie. She tapped me, looked right at me. I could tell she was hoping for an explanation. She had only known me for about eight hours and already she looked to me for answers. I just shrugged.

"It *is*," Mary said. "Yes, it *is* a big deal. These photos are *everywhere*! They're all *over* the place!"

The lady had a point. Aunt June, like most of Dad's family, was into the idea of photos. She probably spent thousands on frames every year. Every wall was covered. And it's true: June was a bit behind the times. What I mean is, a lot of the pictures were from when Dad and Mom were married and I was a baby. I admit I had noticed it myself walking down the hall to the guest room. But like I said, there wasn't much to it. They were pretty much strangers. You know, like the photos that you get when you buy the frame.

But Mary wasn't seeing any of it quite like this. She was talking so loud that I guess Aunt June heard her, because right now she was coming into the room like someone was on fire and asking—

"Is everything all right? Is everything okay?"

"Yeah," Dad said. "All's fine."

"What's wrong?" Melanie said. It didn't matter who she was talking to because no one was listening to her. "Dad what's *wrong*?"

"Sure?" June said.

"Yeah," Dad said again. "All's just fine. We're just tired from the drive," he said. "But, hey, can I talk to you for a second?"

"Oh, of course," June said.

So Dad gets up now, leaves Mary staring at the picture. She was very focused on it, the way some people are in museums when they look at art. I don't mean jackass tourists, or the jackasses who are there just so they have something to talk about at dinner. Mary was like the people who just go and stare at the art, really look at it hard. That's how Mary was, except she was shaking. It was like she wanted to learn something from this picture of my parents. She wanted it to tell her something.

I was kind of glancing at it myself, I admit. I was just sort of curious to see if I'd suddenly remember that day, because I can't really remember anything from when they were together, most of the time I can't even believe any of it really happened at all. I just remember the time at the airport. But they weren't really together then. They were just married.

Dad was whispering something to June now. Her expression changed, got sort of empty looking in this serious way that Dad's family didn't get very often. Then, suddenly, this big smile starts riding her lips and she says—

"Oh, dear, that's not a problem at all."

"What's not?" Melanie said. "Dad, what's not?"

"Are you sure?" Dad asked.

"Of *course* I'm sure," June said.

"Sure about what?" Melanie said.

"Thanks so much," Dad said. "Seriously, thank you."

"Thank you for *what*?"

———

Settled in now, or as close to settled as I figured I'd feel, I decided I'd give Melanie a tour of the house. I hadn't been in that house for years, but I have a pretty flashy memory when it comes to houses, so I knew my way around fine. I figured we could look at all the pictures and I'd tell Melanie about the people in them. I figured it would be a fine way to unwind. Maybe we'd even bond or whatever.

Because of Mary, and her little episode earlier, all the photos of me and Dad and Mom had been turned around. The ones of just Mom had been taken off the walls completely.

So me and Melanie are walking down this hallway, and it was pretty funny what ended up happening. Melanie's stopping at every one of the pictures. She already *knew* everyone in them. She didn't need me to give her any history lessons. My tour was completely foiled. Like right now, when Melanie's looking at a photo of my grandparents, and she's saying—

"Oh *look*, there's Grammy and Grampy! There by the lake next to their house. I *love* Grammy and Grampy! Have you ever been to that lake?"

"I have," I said.

"Grampy took me fishing there once."

"I haven't been since I was like your age," I said. "Catch any fish?"

Grammy and Grampy were pretty old and sick, and didn't make it down from Maine anymore. To this day, the last I've seen of them was when I went up with Mom for

Christmas. But they're still alive. I mean, they sent me that photo of Mike graduating from the military. I really can't get over that he's in the military—

"Oh and look," Melanie was saying, moving on to the next photo. "There's Cousin Will!"

I didn't really mind her ignoring my question. She was just a kid.

"*That's* Will?" I said.

"Will's so funny!" Melanie said. "I love Will!"

It didn't look anything like Will. The last I knew him he was around ten, a few years younger than me. He was one of my favorite cousins, all sorts of scrappy, with this bright orange hair, a million freckles. Cousin Mike had stopped coming up to Maine completely because he was pretty much a full blown delinquent drug addict. Stacey didn't come anymore either, because she'd stopped talking to Ray and the rest of the family too.

That was it with them, so if you want to know more I'm sorry.

But back in the day when Mike used to come up, me, him, and Will would go to the lake by Grammy and Grampy's, to catch frogs, of all things. I mean, if you met me now you'd never think I was the type of guy who grew up catching frogs at a lake in Maine. You'd maybe even think I was doing my homework all the time or whatever. But that's exactly what we did. We'd catch them, then throw them out into the water far as we could. It wasn't as boring as it sounds. They'd hit the water and just lay there, all stunned. Then you'd see these ripples around them. They were moving again. You knew they were okay.

But in this photo Will was a teenager, tall as hell, pretty strong-looking too. I didn't really care that he looked so different—I know what growing up means. It was that I realized I hadn't even thought about Will's existence at all for years. I have a little theory that we are all constantly concerned about the existence of about a hundred people in the world at any given moment. Half of them tend to be people we don't know, like movie stars and politicians and the people our friends tell us about who we never meet, like who they're dating for ten minutes or whatever. Then there's a few slots for the people right around you, a limited supply, for friends and the family you see all the time. And then there's a slew of slots that are supposed to go to people like Will, but I guess his had already been taken by someone else, someone I hadn't yet met. Anyway, I guess it's these slots that are for people like Dad too, or else I wouldn't be going on about him like this, considering I barely ever knew him. I don't know. Right there I just wanted to see him so bad, Will I mean. My mouth felt sour. I almost felt guilty.

"Will's one of my *favorites*!" Melanie was saying. "Do you know Will? I *love* Will!"

"You know Will?" I asked. "I can't believe *you* know Will?"

"Of course," she said. "Will's my cousin."

"You know," I said, "he's actually not."

"Huh?"

"Your cousin, I mean. Will's not your cousin."

But with all these pictures before her, she couldn't really focus on what I was saying. She had that kind of mind. You could put Melanie on the couch, turn on the television, sit down next to her, and start talking and she wouldn't even notice. You could probably start cutting your wrists all up. You could be screaming and getting blood all over the place, and she'd just be staring at some cartoon like a blind man.

That explains her now saying—

"It's Grammy again! Look, it's Grammy! I *love* Grammy!"

"No," I said. "It isn't."

"Oh and look!" she said, going on to another picture. "Look at this one! Look at how *young* he is!"

"That's not your grandmother," I said.

"He's so *young*!" Melanie said. "You almost don't know who it is. Look at him!"

I figured I'd stop trying to correct her petty grasp on genealogy, and humor her by looking at this next photo, the one she was all hung up on.

God, he did look young—

Melanie was right about that, but it wasn't hard to tell who it was. I didn't think so at least.

"*Look* at him!"

It was T.J., of all people.

He was around twelve years old. You knew it was him because his skin was tan, his eyes exactly the same, big and brown, with those long lashes. After all that fun went down with him I hadn't really thought about him at all. It's funny. I mean, there was that shrink everyone made me see, the one with all that hair coming out of his ears. But I never brought it up, and whenever he tried to I just lied about something else that was going on. He'd say do you want to tell me about T.J., and I'd tell him I was thinking about trying cocaine. I'd never touch cocaine, but it always distracted him. I think Mom had given him a little debriefing on our family history. Don't ever go to a shrink, though. Like a lot of adults, they just make everything up, and some of it stays with you longer than you think.

"I love T.J. too!" Melanie was saying.

"You know T.J.?" I asked.

"Of course," Melanie said. "He's my cousin. He came over to our house once." She was so excited, speaking in this way where she wasn't necessarily answering me but just talking out loud and saying things that happened to work as responses. You know, how nine year olds do. "He stayed for a few weeks, a while ago," she was saying. "We had so much fun!"

"That's crazy that you know T.J.," I said. "Do you even know who your father is?"

"It was great!"

"Do you?"

"Did you know T.J. went to *jail*?" Melanie said. "But him and Dad said he was framed, like in that *Roger Rabbit* movie. Have you seen that movie?"

That's how I found out about his getting arrested. It's still all I know. Funny, right? Some things, you just don't want to ask about.

"It was just like having an older brother!" Melanie said.

I guess this last statement of hers jarred her into remembering that I was right next to her. Because she turned to me now, took my hand. Then she looks up at me, and do you know what she says?

"And now *you're* my older brother because we have the same dad."

———

I understand she was nine, and because of that she was stupid when it came to things like this. But it wasn't like I was so logical myself. I mean, I'm twenty now, and I barely know anything. And I was only seventeen then, and had just spent a six-hour drive hearing Melanie calling him Dad the whole way. And now this. I just wasn't up for acting like such an adult anymore. So I let go of her hand, but kept looking right into her.

"No," I politely said. "We don't."

"What?" she asked.

"We do not have the same father," I said.

"Yes we do," Melanie said.

"Trust me, darling," I said. "I am not your brother and in some corridor of your little infantile mind you comprehend this."

I liked talking like this sometimes. Sometimes it would really have an effect. Like when a teacher was annoying me, and I'd get up in front of the class and go after them, talking smarter than I ever was in any paper I wrote.

But when it's a nine year old girl you're talking to, it just doesn't make any sense to her.

"I don't get it," Melanie said.

"Look," I said. "These pictures, these people in them, they are *not* your family. Okay? Do you hear me now? None of these people knows who you are. Your father is some *lunatic,* Dad told me," I said. "I'm going to the bathroom now."

———

I didn't really need to use the bathroom. I just wanted to get away from Melanie. I didn't even turn on the light. I had started doing stuff like this ever since I got into high school, when I was really upset, which I guess was like all the time. Like I'd be brushing my teeth and all of a sudden I was using the toothbrush on my fingernails, really going at them, brushing hard, rinsing them in the water, just like they were my teeth. One time I was playing Nintendo and when I lost a level of some stupid game—I think it was Zelda—I got so angry I tried to knock the wind out of myself. Another time I was walking this dog me and Mom had then. His name was Dundee, and he's dead now. Anyway, I was walking him and I can't remember what he did exactly, just something normal for dogs. Like when they zone out and forget to come even though you asked them to ten times. Dundee did something like that and it made me so livid I ended up kicking him in the gut. I kicked him hard as I could, this poor dog. And let me just tell you, if you ever want to feel like the world's supreme jackass, try kicking your dog in the gut hard as you can. He barely even whimpered.

Sometimes, I'd be standing around, and it would just piss me off how still I could stand, if that makes any sense to you. I'd feel my legs on the ground, could feel how strong they were, the muscles in them so indestructible, and it made me so angry, because I just sort of wanted to collapse. So I'd think real hard about collapsing and it would happen. I guess if you ever happened to walk in on one of these sessions you'd just say I fainted, passed out for a second. Or you'd think maybe I was crazy. But it was much more controlled than that. I swear.

———

In the bathroom now I was just looking at myself in the mirror, but with the lights off and my eyes closed. And I guess I was thinking about how easy it was for me to stand, how perfectly my leg muscles functioned, because when I opened my eyes I was on the floor, the ceiling staring at me like it was about to fall and kill me. I could tell I hadn't been down there too long, so I just got up, flushed the toilet so anyone listening would think I had just gone to the bathroom. Then I came out, and Melanie was still right there in the hall where I left her. She was staring at that picture still, the one of T.J.

"Hey, you okay?" I said.

"I don't understand," Melanie was saying. "I don't understand."

"Hey, there," I said.

"I don't understand."

"Hey, relax. Don't worry about it. And don't *cry* for God's sake."

"But you said—"

"I know, I know," I said. "I'm sorry."

But actually, I wasn't sorry at all. Maybe you think I should have been, but I swear if you were there you'd understand. It's not like I haven't regretted how I acted since. But right then I just wanted to make sure she understood everything I meant.

"But—"

"Look, it's true," I said. "It just is. These people are *my* family, not yours."

"*D-A-A-A-D!*" she was suddenly yelling, like I had tried to hurt her or something. "*D-A-A-A-D—*"

"Hey there," I said. I was covering her wet mouth now. God, her teeth really were messed up, like Cro-Magnon or something. You should have felt how wet and snotty my palm was. Sometimes I still think about it. You know, like when I'm washing my hands. "Do you want me to explain this to you or not? Or do you just want to act like a baby and yell for some dad who's not even yours?"

"I don't know," she said.

"Exactly," I said. "You don't have a clue. But look, I'll explain it all to you. I'll straighten you out."

―――――

So we were in another room now, the one me and Melanie would be sharing. It had two beds. I was on one, and she was on the other. She had calmed down now. I'm actually good with kids, if you really want to know. I can calm them down real easy.

You should have been there. I was so thorough with her, with my explanation of why none of the people in those precious photos had anything to do with her. I was very formal, very professional and polite. I started at the beginning, with the basics.

"Do you know how babies are made?" I asked.

"Sort of," she said.

"You don't know, do you?" I said.

"I don't know."

"Well, it's like this . . . ," I began.

And I didn't hold back. I wish you were there. You should have seen me. I was a star. I wasn't vague in the least. I mean, I gave her *all* the details. I was like a doctor with the details. I avoided euphemisms, and fielded her questions like a professor. It really wasn't so ridiculous. It felt like a very natural thing, my speaking like this. Sometimes I swear I could be a truly great teacher.

Melanie listened very intently, found a lot of it very amusing. Like when she said—

"There's really *white* stuff?"

"It's more translucent than white," I said.

"What's tranzluchent?" she asked.

"Like white, but kind of see-through," I said. "But that's not the point here," I said. "We're getting off subject."

"And that's where the, um, *babies* are?" she asked. "*In* the white stuff?"

"That's where half of them are," I said. "Good job."

I was starting to feel close with her. I just loved how she was listening so carefully to what I was saying. I couldn't think of anyone else really who ever had. It was like she was a good friend of mine, someone my own age who just happened not to know about the specifics of procreation. That's what I mean about getting along with kids. A lot of the time talking to them is just like talking to someone my own age.

But like with all kids, it turned out she hadn't really been listening to my little sermon, not like an adult I mean. Because after explaining the physical end of things, I went into all the legal stuff, about marriage and how you can have lots of different families depending on how many times your parents end up married. I made sure she understood that these were *not* real families. This was very important to me. I must have said this twenty times.

That's why I would've paid someone to knock me out when I finally finished everything, and the first thing out of Melanie's wet little mouth showed she hadn't heard a thing—

"But can you still be my brother?" she asked.

———

God, was I upset. This girl had no learning curve. And her face looked so lost. I mean, look at it: all adorable in that way I couldn't deal with right now.

So, in response, I resorted to the kind of muddled and senseless statement that only a nine year old would comprehend. I had that sour feeling in my mouth again, and my eyes felt dry. If you really want to know, I was crying.

But I just wanted her to shut up so I could go to sleep

and wake up and drive back to Maryland by myself at ninety miles an hour. It's all I wanted.

"I'm only your brother if I agree to it," I said. "It's up to me, and I choose not to."

She just looked at me now. Her mouth was so wet. So were her eyes. I had to get out of there. She was about to explode and I didn't know what I'd do.

"I am *not* your brother," I said. "Got it?"

———

Dad's talking to me now.

It was the next day, at night. Easter was tomorrow. We were going to go to church. I hadn't been inside a Catholic church since I was around seven, when me and Dad were all about going to bars together. I had almost forgotten that half of me was Catholic, at least in theory. Mom's side is Jewish, but none of them really believes it. They're smart types, I told you, so when my grandparents were literally *in* the Holocaust, they took this as a cue to find better things to believe in than God and salvation. Anyway, I know they're supposed to be beautiful, but I just hate the inside of churches, synagogues too, any houses of worship actually.

We had spent the day with a lot of the family, and it had been pretty nice seeing them. Mary was in bed now, and we were having a beer together, just me and Dad. I don't think I had really talked to him the whole trip—there was too much noise everywhere. He was all quiet right now. So was the house. I could tell he had a lot on his mind. He just had that face.

"What's up?" I asked.

"Feller," he said, "I wanna talk about some things."

"What's that?"

"Some of the things you said to Melanie last night."

"What do you mean?"

"I think you know."

It was strange how fatherly he sounded. He never sounded like this. What bothered me was that it managed to feel parental anyway, like he was actually going to be right in whatever he said.

"Oh come on, Dad," I said. "It doesn't matter."

"No," he said. "It does matter."

I took a sip of my beer.

"I was just kidding around with her. And it's not like I was even lying."

"That's not the point."

"Well then, what's the point?" I said.

"It's just not funny, feller," Dad said.

I took another sip of my beer. There was something about his statement that got to me. It was just that the older I got the more things around me seemed to be funny. I swear, some days it's like every single thing around me is just there to make me laugh.

"But Dad," I said, "everything's funny."

"Some things are not funny," Dad said.

"Oh come *on*," I said. "You've got a sense of humor. *This* is even funny, this conversation right here."

"Some things just aren't funny," he said again.

"But you see, that's where our outlooks diverge," I said. I told you I'd started talking like this sometimes. "That's where the chasm is," I now said. "But there's humor there. If you look attentively you'll see there's humor to be excavated."

"What are you saying?"

"Just that it's so funny," I said. "That's all."

"Listen," Dad said to me now. "It's just not funny."

He was so damn parental. You would have never believed that for a living this man sliced meat at a place called the Ding Dong Deli. You'd have thought he was a lawyer or something.

"No Dad," I said. "It is. I swear. You shut up and listen to me. I promise you. It doesn't matter. It's hysterical. It's funny as hell."

I think he said something in response, but it's not like I was paying attention. I got up, said goodnight, went to the bathroom. Don't worry, I turned on the lights this time. And eventually I was driving home by myself, which was incredible, the white lines flying under the car like they were being sucked into a vacuum. And what's really funny was how fast the next year went by without me and Dad saying one thing to each other. I always liked thinking about how we were so disconnected that if some angry lunatic one day happened to shove one of those little oyster forks into Dad's left eye, and Dad ended up blind, I wouldn't even know about it. I'd have a blind father and wouldn't even know it. Because when he did finally call me up, he didn't even know if he should call himself Dad or Joe. He was very confused. He mumbled, and then sat still on the other line for a second. It was funny. He ended up settling on Joe.

BLOOD RELATIVES

told you how Mary was always going crazy, how she was about to lose it all the time. It turned out that she was always pregnant. That's why she was such a nut. Dad was always getting her pregnant, and she kept having miscarriages. It happened something like five times in one year. She'd be all crazed and frantic, then she'd eventually head to the doctor, find out she was knocked up. Then she'd get home and pee blood into the toilet. And then she'd collapse on the tile floor, with her underwear all knotted up around her ankles. She was one of these blind-faith Catholics, so for her, having a miscarriage, tragically natural as it is, was right up there with having an abortion. It was a sin. That's why Mary would cry for a week straight. That's why she was always crying.

This is what Dad's telling me about right now—

We were on the phone. This was the first time we had talked since that stellar Easter vacation. He sounded all solemn, which didn't fit. Dad's the type of guy who handles depression much better by doing something along the lines of standing up on a table and jumping in a pile of brie cheese. I almost couldn't take any of it seriously. It was like he was telling me about the secondary plot of some movie he'd seen ten years ago, certainly not his girlfriend's miscarriages. It's funny. Whenever you go a long time without talking to someone who used to matter to you, a lot of pointless things are said, just to fill some kind of space.

"That's something," I was saying. This was about the tenth time I'd said this during the conversation, and we'd only been on the phone maybe ten minutes.

"Yeah, feller," Dad said. God, he sounded so dismal. It was painful to hear. "It sure is, isn't it?"

"I mean are you—you know?" I said. "*Using* anything?"

"It's pretty crazy, huh?" he said.

I figured it was safe to take this as a no. After all, Mary was a practicing Catholic, so I guess it was a lame question.

"It's something," I said.

I figured the reason Dad was telling me about all these miscarriages, and about Mary all balled up on the bathroom floor, was because he was embarrassed at how Mary was that one time I met her, at Easter. I thought I understood where Dad was coming from. I mean, no one wants the people he respects to think he's dating some crazy woman who can barely even look at a stupid photograph or finish a complete sentence because she's always about to start crying.

But this was all wrong. Dad's solemn explanation, this rare phone call. It was not an issue of pride. It had nothing to do with an interest in historical accuracy. I mean, the guy may have sounded like he was about to commit suicide, but he was calling to share with me some glorious news.

"But this time," he was now saying, "it looks like we're in the clear."

"What's that?" I said.

"That there won't be any complications this time around."

Of course I knew what he meant. I wasn't three. But that mechanism we all have went off inside me. You know, where you just want to be so stupid that you don't understand anything that's happening around you.

"What?"

In a strange way, I just wanted to hear him say it, very

clearly, and not just because I knew it would kill him to say it, but because I knew it would sort of kill me too, if that makes any sense.

"What?" I said again.

"I know, feller," he said. "It's somethin', isn't it?"

"Wait a second here."

"It's true."

"Wait a second," I said. "I zoned out for a minute. What's true? What are we talking about?"

"Mary," Dad said. "She's pregnant."

"Mary is pregnant." I was right: it did sort of kill me. I hate how I'm always so right. "And I hate to ask," I said, "but you're sure that this time it's—"

"Yeah," he said. "She's almost due. About two more months."

"No shit," I said. "That's something."

"I know, feller."

"That's really something."

"You're gonna have a little brother," Dad said.

———

I was a senior in high school now, in my last semester, actually going to New York City for college in the fall, Hunter College, which may not sound like much to you but I was pretty psyched. Anyway, all through high school I hadn't really had a girlfriend. I mean, there was Claudia for a while, but that was sort of spillover from middle school so I don't really count it. But don't get me wrong. I wasn't that kid hanging out in the corner, hair growing out of his palms, waiting for the blisters all over his face to disappear so people could see that he was actually a human being and not the forgotten remains of some petri dish experiment. If you were that kid, I'm sorry. I hope you're better now. Most people seem to improve.

Me, I went out with lots of girls, kissed almost all of them. I don't want to sound arrogant, but I swear by that last year I had pretty much kissed every good-looking girl in the school. I was lucky that way. I was sort of a fuckup, and if there's one mystery about girls it's how they're all kind of obsessed with getting with the fuckup. I mean, I had even kissed most of the ugly ones too. You know, the kind who are geniuses when it comes to trying to be pretty.

I can tell you stories, that's what I'm getting at here. Like about when I was a junior and me and this senior girl started fooling around. Her name was Traci—"with an *i*, not a *y*!"—and she was one of these really great-looking people who you hate because you know her personality will only continue to disintegrate the longer she lives and, alas, you blink once and suddenly she's ugly as hell. She was preppie and popular, could often be found wearing a sweatshirt with some college's insignia smeared all over it, leftover from some older ex-boyfriend who probably didn't even really like her. She had these very tan legs, even in winter. They were so smooth in that high-school-girl way. You now, where you weren't sure if she was an all-star with the Gillette, or if she just didn't have any hair follicles below her neckline. One look at Traci, and I swear all you wanted was to mummify her in Fruit Roll-ups.

But she's not even worth going into. The only reason I brought her up was because of this one time we were fooling around. Mom was out of town, so me and Traci were up in her room, up on Mom's fancy bed, pretty much having sex, except that all our clothes were on. So I guess you could say we were just making out, but I've never been too big on those kinds of details. My hands were on her ass the whole time, because, trust me, if there was any reason to put up with Traci it was because there was a chance of getting your hands on her ass. And, anyway, because of the motion, you know, the grinding or whatever, I ended up skinning my knuckles. Because of the friction against the sheets. They didn't bleed, just scabbed over the next day, like some fool had tried to polish them with a Brillo Pad.

And the really funny part is that two days later I was doing the exact same thing with this other girl, Tanya, who was sort of heinous but kind of attractive in that way prudish girls can be when they're trying to fake like they're sluts. So we're going at it, in Tanya's little bedroom, on Tanya's little twin bed. It was in the afternoon, before her mother got home—like everyone else, her parents were divorced too, never really around. We were on her pink sheets, when all of a sudden she's flipping out because there's these streaks of blood all over the place. We'd ripped off the scabs. You should have been there. You would have cracked up, I swear.

"How'd the cuts get there anyway?" she asked.

She was on top of me now, holding my hands and looking at them. She was looking at the palms though. Girls are always looking at your palms, acting all whimsical, if you haven't noticed.

"Oh I don't know," I said. "Sometimes I cut my knuckles when I get real upset."

"*Seriously?* That's kind of—"

"No, I'm kidding," I said. "I fell down the stairs and got a real bad carpet burn."

It's amazing, the lies you can get away with. That's the problem with me, I'm always telling these sort of half lies to people. She was pretty cool with it though, actually didn't want to stop. Tanya was obsessed with reading three-quarters of every one of those stupid Anne Rice vampire books, so she was conditioned to think the blood was sexy. The girl wanted to roll around in it.

"We can pretend I'm on my period," I said.

That got her. She didn't want to mess around anymore, or really even talk to me ever again. I don't know why, but

I was always saying things like that to girls back then. It's not all that different now.

———

So I'd never had a girlfriend. And if you really want to know, I didn't really like fooling around with girls that much. I don't mean I was gay. They just all seemed so stupid, at least all the good-looking ones. And I don't mean it sexist, because most of the guys were just as stupid, so really it was kind of amazing that anyone took the time to hook up with anyone. I mean, everyone around me was flat-out *dumb*. Things like this don't bother me so much anymore, but back then I wasn't so smart. Once you realize that most of the people around you are jackasses, you stop caring about whether they like you or not.

At the time I'd just get with girls because I was constantly curious about why I didn't like it. For me it was always a sort of experiment, where I was both constant and variable. I would just never let them do anything to me, never really let them touch me. I'd do all sorts of things to them, anything they'd let me really. And if they ever tried to reciprocate, which high school girls are always doing, attacking you like it's a sacred mission, I had a pretty genius plan. It went a little something like this:

"Oh no," I'd say. "Don't. You don't have to."

"You don't *want* me to?"

"No, it's not that, I just—"

"Do you not like me? Do you think I'm *fat*?"

"No, it's that I like you so much."

"Shut up."

"No really," I'd say. "It's sort of embarrassing. I mean, I didn't want to say anything."

"What do you mean?"

"Just that I—God, it's embarrassing—but I just, um, actually *got off*. You know, when I was doing that to you."

"No way! Really?"

"I swear. Really."

"Well, I *could* sort of feel it. Now that I think about it."

"Yeah," I'd say. "I thought you could."

Does this make me a criminal? All I'd do is wait for them to leave, and then I'd take care of that element for real, their reciprocation, when I was alone. And if you want to know something truly perverted, I still thought about Claudia most every time. Claudia in the woods. Claudia in some Gap dressing room, that dark skin of hers all bare and goosebumped. Claudia and her thin brown mouth. Claudia on the phone that night telling me exactly what to do. Claudia when she'd still talk to me, when she looked at me in the halls. Claudia accepting my apology, and me still saying I'm sorry, I'm so sorry. Claudia telling me don't worry, it's okay, it's fine. Actually, I still think about Claudia quite a bit. That way, I mean. When I'm alone.

Mom was always working, but she was cool in that she made sure we ate together as much as possible. She just didn't cook too many of the meals. Instead, the people who worked at Hunan Palace just off North Washington Street ended up cooking and delivering a lot of dinners for us. They probably fed us four days a week. The other three we went out to restaurants because Mom was making cash now and could afford it. I liked this kind of lifestyle, because I thought it was more urban, and since I was soon moving up to New York I was especially into the idea of being as urban as possible.

Right now me and Mom were eating Hunan Palace, on the living room couch, using the ottoman as our dining room table. This is how we always ate, even though we had a real dining room just on the other side of the kitchen. The dining room table was just too big or something. All those empty seats made you lose your appetite.

We were watching *Jeopardy!*, munching on pork dumplings fried on both sides, General Tso's chicken, and who knows what else that you'll never find for real in China. A commercial was on, and pretty much out of nowhere I announced—

"Dad called me today."

She always handled everything with Dad all professional, only a few times did she lose it, like that time I told you about when she went off about the cocaine. Sometimes I look at Dad now and wonder why I actually like the guy at all, and I guess it's because Mom stepped back and let me get to know him on my own. I asked her about this once, not too long ago, asked her why you even let me see the guy. "Well, he is your father, and I wanted you to be as close to him as possible." That's all she said.

It's pretty amazing, I think. Some parents—like the parents of half my friends—put their kids through such ridiculous shit that the kids will never be able to take themselves seriously as adults. A lot of these kids are adults now, so trust me. I know what I'm talking about. Parents like that should be shot. Problem is, they're more than half this country.

"Get out," Mom was now saying. "How long had it been?"

"Like more than a year," I said. "A while."

"Wow."

"I know," I said. "He didn't know if he should call himself Dad or Joe."

"You're kidding?"

"Seriously," I said. "He ended up settling on Joe."

Mom was laughing hard now. So was I. Me and Mom were pretty close, real close, like so close I don't want to talk about her too much here, don't want to taint her like that.

Anyway, we could find humor in stuff like this. Like how I used the twenty-five-dollar money order Dad gave me every year for my birthday to take Mom out to dinner on Father's Day.

"He settled on *Joe!*" Mom was saying.

"I know!" I said.

"*I* don't even think of him as Joe anymore!" she said.

We just sat there laughing. Me and Mom together were always laughing, when I think about it. It's the same today.

Jeopardy! came back on now and we both got quiet. We were pretty involved in the show, even though neither of us would have really wept if someone came along and euthanized Alex Trebek. Mom was an expert at the show, real smart, and I wasn't so bad myself, considering I barely got passing grades. I was really genius at geography. I really like maps, just staring at them, especially memorizing bodies of water. Me and Mom's big, hilarious inside joke revolved around this time that I knew that one of the Final Jeopardy answers was the Strait of Dardanelles (which goes into the Aegean Sea, in case you ever want to sound smart). What's funny is that's why I did bad in school, because I spent half my time making sure I knew exactly where places like the Strait of Dardanelles were, like I had this big trip planned or something.

Another commercial came on now, and it hit me that I had left out another funny detail from the conversation with Dad. I figured me and Mom could have another good laugh.

"Oh yeah," I said. "Know what else? About Dad?"

"What's that?" Mom said. "Did he call you 'sir'?"

"No, seriously," I said.

"What's that?"

"You know Mary?" I said.

"His wife?"

"They're not married," I said. "But she *is* having a baby. Mary is pregnant."

Mom's all quiet for a minute, not really laughing at all, and not really seeming like she was about to anytime soon. She was quiet in a real pensive way. It's funny. I've noticed that single moms can all get quiet in the exact same way. It kind of kills you to watch.

"Wow," she finally said. But she didn't sound all that enthusiastic.

"I know," I said. "Mary is pregnant."

The show came back on, but right now neither of us was particularly dying to watch it.

"God," Mom was saying. "Are they getting married?"

"I guess," I said. "I think he said something about that. I feel pretty bad for Dad."

That was the thing. I really *did* feel bad for him. I mean, I had a pretty great gig going on, with this great house and this nice car and a cool mother, and part of that could have been his. That's how I got to thinking about Dad, and his life up in Jersey. I guess for a little while there I had been sort of angry, that Easter trip being a prime example, but I'm the type of person who can't stay angry that long. It tires me out.

See, right when Dad told me that Mary was pregnant, right when I realized he'd probably have to get married to this sort of frantic woman and live with her kid Melanie forever, I just felt bad for him. Like one day he'll be dead, and all the wrong people will show up at his funeral. There was no getting around it. Dad's life up there was a wreck. It was the exact kind of life that nobody wants. And now he had to keep on living it.

"*He* got himself into it," Mom was saying.

"Yeah I know," I said. "But it just sucks for him up there. I mean, you should see it. It's this dirty little house in this weird area."

"Your father and I once lived in a dirty little house in a weird area, before you were born."

"Yeah, whatever. That kid Melanie is probably the worst kid in the world, and he has to deal with her calling him Dad all the time. And Mary, I told you how she freaked out when she saw that photo of you and Dad. I don't know. I just feel bad for him."

"It's amazing," Mom said.

"Yeah, it's crazy."

"No," Mom said. "It really is amazing how forgiving you are."

"Oh yeah," I said. "I forgot something else."

"There's more?"

"Well, it's really nothing."

"What is it?"

"The baby," I said. "They know it's going to be a boy."

"Wow," Mom said. "You'll have a little half brother."

"I know," I said. "It's wild."

"It really is. It's really something."

"But that's not what I wanted to say," I said.

"Well?"

"This kid," I said. "Dad wants to name him after me."

———

That last year of high school there was this one girl I was interested in. Her name was Liz, and she was one of these new students who come from out of nowhere and disintegrates the tiny reserve of common sense in every single boy in the school. She looked about twenty-five, dressed like a woman in a magazine, in these short sexy skirts, bright stockings, funky tight shirts, clunked-out boots, the laces crossing ten thousand times. Sometimes around her wrist you'd see a spiky bracelet. She was tall and skinny, had a strut in her walk, also like the people who make it into magazines. And she was always reaching into her backpack, or fixing her shoe, or putting a clip in her black hair in just the right way that her top would drift up and you'd see a little bit of her stomach, the knobs of her pelvic bone, or her lower back, which in my opinion is a woman's strongest feature. Basically, I'm not lying or being at all subjective when I say that Liz was the best looking girl to come to any high school in any American town in 1998. You know that way football types talk about girls, like all obsessive, the same way criminals talk about God? Well that's how *everyone* talked about Liz.

And right now I was kissing her—

She was very forward and direct—you could tell it was sort of her thing. And today after school she had come up to me like—

"I'm into your car. You should give me a ride."

She was sort of contrived, I admit, like an eighties movie. But I didn't care.

"Where?" I asked.

"I don't care," Liz said. "To the courthouse, to a graveyard."

I was only eighteen, so I thought this was about the most amazing thing anyone had ever said to me. I didn't take her to any courthouse or graveyard though, not right away at least. I went out Falls Road, because it was sort of countrylike and peaceful, driving fast, all show-offy around the curves, downshifting like I was some NASCAR expert, the low branches of the trees pretty much slamming against the windshield.

She was from Texas, San Antonio. She told me this during the ride. She was just here for a year, because her stepfather had to do some work in Rockville, something like that. It's not like she had that accent or anything, but I now attributed some of that strut and that spunk of hers to being from Texas.

After whipping around through Falls Road, I came back out where we started, right at our high school. Drive on a lot of the roads in Rockville and it's a funny thing: you just end up right where you started. I drove across the street where there was this church, like over a hundred years old, with a cemetery behind it.

"A graveyard after all," Liz said, her arm wrapped through mine, like we were about to get married as we walked over to the graves.

Everything Liz said was interesting. You know what I mean? Like she could have said hello, and you'd be like I can't believe a girl who looks like you says hello like that. She could have wiped something from her cheek, and you wished you had a video camera, so people would believe that you were once out with a girl who wiped something from her cheek like that. I mean, you just expected her to turn into a cloud of smoke and be gone. You were waiting for it. I think that about pretty much every girl I meet that

I'd consider marrying. That they're about to turn into a cloud of smoke and vanish at any second.

"This place is fucking great," she said.

"You gotta see this one grave," I said. "It's pretty funny."

"Jesus," she said when we got to it. I realized it was dark out now, because Liz's face, the way it was silver all of a sudden when I looked at her, meant the streetlights were all on. I barely knew her, but already I liked to gauge pretty much everything around me using her face. "He's really famous. What's he doing buried *here*?"

"We read his book in English sophomore year," I said.

"Yeah, so did we."

"Everybody in the world does I think. Like, really everybody, like in Japan even, millions," I said. "I didn't really like it."

"Whatever," Liz said. "I never read the fucking books in class. What's it about?"

"I guess that's what I meant," I said. "I didn't read it either."

I now realize how hysterical it is, that he's buried in Rockville of all places, because I've read his book since and get the joke now. I mean you've got to understand, Rockville's an old town, but unlike all those little shady hamlets you've got polluting New England, no one ever cared about preserving Rockville, so every ten years since the beginning it's been plowed over, reinvented. By the time I was ever alive this just meant redoing the facades of the million stripmalls lining Rockville Pike so they'd look fancier, because people kept getting richer. We watched Congressional Plaza, Richie Center, Wintergreen, all once gaudier than a heavily made-up corpse, get turned into these pastel-colored structures that were very soothing to stare at. It was like whoever designed them knew that families would spend their lifetimes in these parking lots, going in and out of these stores, and wanted to create a building so fantastically boring that no one noticed it was really there. That way, when they tore it down, and put up another, no one would get sentimental.

But at the start of the Pike, before all this, there's this one little section, where this church was, where you could see that Rockville did actually exist before 1975, that it was actually once a quaint little place. And then you get to this grave, and you see that F. Scott Fitzgerald, of all people, is stuck rotting under this ground, right across the street from my high school, in the shadow of this mammoth chain furniture store called Marlo, which I swear is listed in Guinness as carrying the world's chintziest sofas. Start at the other end of the Pike, and in only ten minutes you'll drive past three McDonald's, two Roy Rogers, a Bob's Big Boy, four 7-Elevens, nine Foot Lockers, one Bennigan's, the T.G.I. Friday's across the street, the Ruby Tuesday next door, all these plastic signs, and at the end of it you get to this skuzzy graveyard and F. Scott Fitzgerald, a guy even il-literates recognize as a famous writer. I'm not even kidding. You should really go and see it because I guarantee one day soon they'll plow right over it. Like I said, they're always plowing over things like this in Rockville.

"Why are there all those packs of cigarettes and bottles of liquor around his grave?" Liz was asking.

"I don't know," I said. "I think because he was a real drunk and now that he's dead people love him for it."

"That's so typical. My real dad's a drunk, but he's still alive."

"Yeah, mine is too, but I never see him anymore."

"Maybe that's better," she said. "Do you drink?"

"Yeah," I said. "Not that much, though."

"Well, we should come out here some night, to this grave, bring a bottle of vodka."

"Sure," I said. I mean, it seemed like a fine idea. I've never been too big a drinker, because of Dad and all, but it's not like I'm against it either. "Wanna get out of here?"

———

So we get in my car, and like three minutes later, we're parked up in front of her house, this little townhouse de-velopment, and we're kissing. The way she was sort of crazed, kind of frantic—it made her one of these girls who sort of laughs while kissing you. Normally I hate that, because you never know what the hell they're finding so funny, but I didn't mind at all with Liz.

And then, like I had bit her or something, she suddenly pulled away.

"Hey, tell me something that happened to you this week," she said, all urgent. But she could say something like this and it seemed normal still.

"Okay," I said. "My Dad just got some woman pregnant and wants to name the kid after me."

"That's fucking hilarious," she said.

"I know," I said. I loved her for saying this. It was right when she said it that I knew she'd go away. No real girl would ever say something like that and stick around. "My Mom lost it," I said. "She called him up and threatened to sue, because he hasn't paid child support ever. She was so pissed."

"I *love* it!" she said. "Your mom sounds amazing."

"Oh, she is," I said. "Yours?"

"She's not so brilliant," Liz said. "Better than my real dad, though. He used to beat the shit out of me!"

"What was the worst thing he ever did?"

It's funny, how absurd these kinds of conversations seem all of a sudden. Especially when you realize that you were having them all the time.

"I don't really know," she said. "Let me think. He used to do this thing where he'd make me kneel on uncooked rice, with my arms sticking out. It kills your knees."

"That's fucking sick."

"Like Jesus at a wedding, right?" she said.

"Jesus."

"He's really not that bad," she said. "Only when he's doing that shit. He's just always doing it, so I never see him."

"My Dad was just always asleep," I said. "I barely knew him."

"You're lucky," she said. "Trust me."

"He changed the name, my Dad did, of the baby," I said. "My legacy's shot now, huh?"

But instead of answering me she just wrapped her hand around my neck, her fingers running up into the back of my hair, her lips coming at me now like nothing in the world was funny anymore, like every single joke had been told. I think I told you how I had started to dislike girls touching me, how it made me feel like they just wanted me to start telling them lies. But Liz seemed lost and crazy enough not to care about what lies I had to tell.

She pulled away again, looked at the clock, its red digital numbers the brightest thing in the car, looked me right in the face now.

"Fuck," she said. "I gotta run."

"I knew it," I said.

"We need to get this over with, and soon," she said. "Tell your mom I say hi, okay?"

———

I don't think it completely registered, what she meant by this, not until the next night, when at two in the morning Liz snuck over to my house and we were in my room, mouths lit up and burning with vodka, and she was on her back on my floor, laughing, her teeth flashing glossy and white, and I was kneeling, sliding her jeans off.

It was the first thong underwear I'd ever seen that wasn't in a magazine. I didn't really know what I was doing, but with the vodka making knots out of the veins that go to my brain, I didn't really care. I mean, I had been naked with a girl before, but never in a way that I expected to actually have sex. It's funny. I've had sex since, and I'm still always shocked it's really happening.

But like I said, my head loose like it was, I wasn't too hung up on any of this right now. Probably because I was so sure Liz was an apparition of sorts, probably because I thought I was making her up. She was just so unreal, it was pretty much like I was all alone—

"Hold on," she was saying. She was always saying something all suddenly like that. "I have to run to the bathroom, to do something."

Based on how quick she was in and out of the bathroom, I could only deduct that she had removed a tampon. This didn't bother me at all. I don't get all disgusted by stuff like that.

"Okay," she said. "Sorry about that."

I pulled her to me, turned her around, because I wanted to see her back. I loved looking at girls' backs, still do. Liz was part Latina or something, the way everyone's part something these days. Her skin had that maize color. Even though the lights were off you could still see this, especially where her scapula bone jutted out. I kissed the back of her neck, her shoulders, right there on her scapula, down her spine to her lower back. I even got into this kind of silly position and kissed behind her knees. She was laughing. I was laughing. I pressed up against her now, still behind her, could feel her hand between my legs now. I was still in my boxers, and she was pulling them down, just enough. She pulled her underwear over to the side, was pulling me closer to her now. Her whole ear was in my mouth, half the hair on her head in my palm, me sort of pulling on it, just barely, not like I wanted to hurt her or anything like that. I just wanted to help her in pulling me closer.

I'd never done this before. I mentioned that, right? This was it. The only thing I was sort of freaked out about was how we weren't using a condom or anything, but to tell you the truth, once we started I wasn't really thinking about any of that. They say the best thing about no condom is how real it feels, but that's not true. It's that without a condom it's much easier to convince yourself that none of it's really happening in the first place.

"Hey, you wanna see something cool?" she was saying now. She was on top of me. We were still on the floor, even though the bed was right there. I was lasting a lot longer than expected, even though I had to keep pushing her away to avoid losing it.

"Sure," I said.

She was still in her bra and underwear, her underwear all stretched off to the side, useless now. I hadn't taken her bra off because I think I mentioned how breasts sort of freaked me out. Even though hers were small, the way I liked, I was still fine with the bra staying on.

But apparently she had a different attitude, because she was taking it off now. What she wanted to show me was her left nipple, which was dark, almost purple. She wanted me to see the bright silver barbell she had pierced through it.

Here is where I'd like to tell you that I held some sort of ideal of Liz as a lost, fucked-up girl, and that it was this barbell running through her nipple that cemented all this. I'd like to admit here that she works well in my memory like that, and I've shortchanged the real woman here, degraded her or whatever. Like in reality she was a well-rounded girl, the kind you probably grew up around, and that I'm ruining her for you. But the fact is she *did* become a stripper, just so you know, dropped out of high school to be called Nikki as she danced half naked up in a neon thong on the stage at Gentleman's, that club on Wisconsin

Avenue in D.C., Georgetown sophomores leaving their Jesuit dorms to spend a night drooling all over her toes. Last I heard she was back in San Antonio, married with a one-year-old son, age twenty-one and looking thirty-five. Just so you understand. Just so you know these people really exist.

But that's all irrelevant, especially right now as I was saying—

"That's cool. Does it hurt?"

"Oh, look," she said. "Are you nervous?"

"What?"

"Your forehead," she said. "It's so sweaty."

"I can't see it."

"Look at mine then," she said. "I'm pretty much you right now."

"Does that thing hurt?"

"No," she said. "You should pull on it."

I wasn't complaining. I gave it a little pull, and she made this noise, something right between a laugh and a whimper. She told me pull a little harder, and I listened. She started moving her hips now, moving them all slow. She was making that sound, that laughing and crying sound, and I had no idea what to do with any of it. I didn't care if she'd been with a thousand other guys. I didn't care about anything. You could forget me tomorrow, and I won't care.

I glimpsed down, saw the blood on the tops of my thighs. I didn't mind. I had my hand on the left side of her hip. Her hips were so trim, almost boyish.

"Okay," she was saying. "Come on, pull even harder."

If she was going to keep saying things like this, if she was going to keep picking up speed like she was doing, I knew I didn't have all that much time left. I mean, it was my first time. And that whole thinking-about-baseball thing—well, let me tell you, it's bullshit.

"Hey," I said. "I'm gonna—"

"Do it inside me," she said. "Do it inside. Please."

She started moving all fast now. Looking at her, at that look in her face, eyes shaking under the lids, cheeks all flushed, I felt lonely all of a sudden. It was like she wasn't even with me anymore, even though she was right there, right there touching all of me—

"Are you sure?"

—touching me in this way where I would have paid someone to cut me open, just so she could look right into me, if you can even get that. Just so you could see me, all of you. Just look at me please. Please. I want all of you to see everything—

"Yeah yeah, it's fine," she was saying.

"Jesus."

"It won't matter. Not now. Jesus. Because I'm you right now," she was saying. "I'm you. We'll do it at the same time," she was saying. "Oh God. Yes. Just pull real hard now. Yeah. Come on just pull—"

Yeah, yeah. It doesn't matter. It does not matter. I'm you. Yes. Jesus. I am you. I am you. I am you. I am you. Please. Please. Just like that, just like that, just like that.

———

I think the thing is, about me, is I just feel bad for pretty much everyone. I don't mean it condescending. For example, after Mom flipped out about Dad wanting to name his son after me, and I realized how pathetic this was, I just felt horrible for Mary, of all people, sorry that now Mary had to live with this man, have a son with him. I thought of her looking at that one picture, the one at Easter from forever ago, with me and Mom and Dad looking like petrified mannequins, like figments from some haggard imagination. I remembered her flipping out. And even though I now got that Mary had been losing it because she was pregnant again, and about to piss it away, it still meant something. Dad wanted to name her kid after the one in the photo, the one that made her insane. I was the one driving her nuts, but still, I couldn't help feeling pity for the woman.

Also, I realize I haven't mentioned any of my friends from high school. I don't know why. Just know I had some close ones. There were some who, for a year—junior year—I was always high with, but then I got bored with drugs and just know that they're still high wherever they are. And then there're the people I'm still in touch with, people with names and faces and all that. People I'm sure you'd love, but they're too precious to be mentioned here.

It's that I'm thinking about Dad now, and when I think about him pretty much everything else goes away. I don't mean in some romantic way—it's just because he's not really attached to any of it. I only saw him like three times through high school, only once since, which I'm about to tell you about. It's funny. When you think real hard about someone who has nothing to do with your life, you just end up forgetting about everything else, the things that matter. Say you're sitting on a bench with a cool girl, a girl you're actually obsessed with, but you just end up looking at all the strangers around you instead of saying anything to her. Wondering all obsessive-compulsive, what's *their* story. Eventually the girl's going to get up, and join them. Trust me.

Anyway, Dad ends up naming it after Uncle Ray, this kid. I guess that's what I was talking about. Little Raymond, my half brother. When the kid was finally born, two months later, I had finished high school. I had actually called up Dad. He was so thrilled. He said the baby was fine. It was eight pounds exactly. Then, because Dad never knows when to be quiet, he said it was just like me. You would have died. Dad couldn't get over this. I mean, he really couldn't shut up about it.

Do you want to hear how he put it?

Looks just like you, he said. He never cries! Just like you, feller! He never cries! Just like you! He really looks just like you, only Filipino!

It was funny. Right as he said this all I wanted was to tell Liz about it. She would have cracked up. It was her type of thing. She would have said that's fucking hilarious. But I didn't talk to Liz anymore, just thought about her too much instead. I never talked to her after that one night. I don't know why exactly. I just didn't talk to her again, and I think I was sort of in love with her, despite how obvious it was what she was about to become. I guess I might just be a little frightened of women. It sounds funny, I know. But I swear a lot of the ones I've known are always trying to bleed all over me.

LUCK?

I wanted to bankrupt the guy. It's true. Dad was like where do you want to go, anywhere you want, and I thought of the most expensive restaurant I knew. It was this seafood place up on Union Square. I'd never been there before, but I knew it had a reputation for being real pricey. They served ten dollar oysters, had supermodel hostesses, things like that. It was the type of place where people go, look over the menu, and then go on about how reasonable the prices are, just because they're that rich and don't know any better.

But I really wasn't interested in any of those kind of frills—actually, for the most part, that kind of thing drives me mad. I don't know why, but I just wanted to sit across from Dad at some fancy table watching him spend more money than he had.

———

You should have seen the guy when he showed up at my apartment. The most perverted minds at Kodak couldn't concoct such a reunion. I buzz him up, open the door, and you just should have seen the guy standing there on the other side.

I mean, Dad started going gray when he was around twenty, but now his whole head was gray. There probably wasn't one of his signature greasy jet-black hairs left. And his moustache—he had shaved it off. So he didn't really look like himself anymore. This was sad. Dad was smiling, but his smile wasn't the same, wasn't his. I was used to seeing his moustache move when he smiled, like it was caught up in some breeze. Now he just had this thin upper lip. It was actually the exact shape as mine, if you want to know the truth.

And he had put on weight. Dad had a paunch now. This was a good thing I guess, because Dad was always thin as hell when I knew him, like you'd give him a hug and your fingers got caught up in his ribcage. But it sort of upset me too, in this funny way. Looking at him, at this slightly over-weight, smiling, gray-haired guy about to enter my apartment, you came to only one conclusion: that this guy was a bona fide father. He had the look down. The whole time I knew him, he always came off just like some guy, a kind of warm, lost, skinny guy with a moustache and a car you were amazed could actually move. I mean, his eyes were still watery, still all cracked with a little pink, but really he just looked like someone who had to pick up the kids at noon. Someone who'd pick them up on time even. It was almost embarrassing.

To be honest, there was this kind of idealistic part of me that was entertaining the notion—had been entertaining it for some time—that I'd open up the door, and me and Dad would give each other this big old hug. You know, like he'd be whispering something poignant in my ear, I'd be telling him I know, I know, he'd be patting my back all tough guy, all that stuff.

But it wasn't like that at all.

He just stood there. That's what he was doing right now, just looking at me blankly, like I was some fascinating zoo animal that he'd heard about but never believed really existed. I was a platypus or whatever, a puffin. This didn't upset me, though. I always figured it must've been weird for Dad, seeing me once every few years, how fast I changed. I mean, for me he was just like a middle-aged guy getting a little more middle-aged, but to him I was a completely different person every time. You could see it in his eyes, how it wasn't really sinking in that this person he was looking at was still actually his son. I felt a little guilty.

But whatever—I come up with idealistic notions like that everyday, mainly with strangers. Like take every good-looking girl I see—there's a part of me that's literally convinced she's about to come over, tap me on the shoulder, and ask me right there to marry her. I'll get so sure of this that I start fretting about the exact way I'm going to say yes, of course, darling, let's go. But then the subway doors always close or whatever.

So Dad's standing there, real still, just looking at me. It was awkward, to say the least. I really had to come up with something genius to say—

"You have no moustache," I said. "Your moustache is gone."

"Yup," Dad said. "Mary says I look younger. I say I just look bald."

"You just look like you don't have a moustache."

"So, this is where you live?"

"Oh yeah," I said. "This is it. Come on in."

————

It had been two years. And the one time we talked in between he was so busy telling me about his new kid, little

Ray, that I forgot to tell him I was going to college. So he actually called up the house in Maryland, and Mom had to explain that I'd moved up to New York, had to give him my address and phone number. I bet that was a fun chat. I mean, they always got on well enough, like they never went at each other in front of me the way my friends' parents did, but still, the last time they'd spoken, Mom was telling him how much of a freak he was for trying to name his love child after me.

So Dad contacted me, with a card. It was pretty much the most hilarious, earnest greeting card you've ever seen. On the front there was a little illustration of a hapless pig, just kind of hanging out on a piece of grass, looking sad as hell. Under him it reads, in that ersatz kiddy handwriting that Hallmark can't get enough of: *I suppose you're wondering why you haven't heard from me lately. I think I can explain . . .* Then you open the thing up and it reads, earnest as hell: *It's because I haven't called or written.*

On the left side, this is what Dad wrote:

It grieves me that we have not spoken for over a year. I don't know what happened other than pure laziness on my part. I miss you and I love you and care about what is going on in your life. How is school? Please call me. I was in Maine for another family reunion in July.

Everyone is asking about you. Your grandparents would like to hear from you. Their health is good, but they are not getting any younger.

Let's talk.

I miss you.

Love,
Dad

I admit it: the thing killed me. It was so expert, so grown-up and mature. I just know that stuff is next to impossible for Dad. It's not an issue of pride or anything. Dad's just deficient in whatever gene it is that allows people to turn into adults as they get older. Call it bad luck if you want. The point is, it would have killed you too, you would have been there just like me, sort of reading the thing and laughing like a psychopath, and then you'd find yourself suddenly going crazy, crying like a legit baby, your face puffed out like there's no tomorrow, just like I was. I mean, especially if you saw the real thing, that greeting card, if you had the chance at seeing Dad's handwriting. It was exactly the same as the one Hallmark used.

I called him right when I got it, or right when I pulled myself together at least. It was a pretty stellar chat. Dad knew exactly who I was, right away. He sounded all depressed. Like I almost didn't know who he was.

He'd be in New York on Sunday, he said. And the thing is, he actually came.

———

"You paint these walls yellow?" Dad was asking.

"That I did," I said. I knew it would impress him, the work I'd done on my apartment. I swear, Dad should have worked at a hardware store—it would have made him the world's happiest man. He can't get enough of fixing things up—like remember that Mercedes? I have a slight knack for it myself I guess, but nothing like Dad. Especially since I really started becoming Mom's kid—I'd just rather call up someone *like* Dad to fix what isn't working, the faucet or whatever. "And the floors, I finished them myself. Not bad, huh?"

"I could never do floors," he said. "Drove me nuts."

"I went a little crazy," I said. "Can you believe that this is actually where I live?"

It was this studio downtown, on the Lower East Side, about the size of a fancy outhouse. I'm still living there, on East Broadway, in this neighborhood where I'm about the only white guy who isn't a Hasidic Jew. It's a pretty sweet location though. Mom knew some wealthy types up in New York, the kind of people who know all the right people, and one of them hooked me up with this sort of permanent, sort of illegal sublet. I think he knew some realtor, or some dead aunt. I can afford the rent, and that's all I really care about. It's funny. Sometimes I look around and I'm convinced everyone in New York lives illegally. At least to some degree.

Anyway, I was going to Hunter College, which I've told you, but what I haven't mentioned is that I had two more years left to get the diploma, and I wasn't so pressed to finish. I decided that the two years I'd had were plenty, and had given notice that I'd be dropping out, which they reworded as a leave of absence. I found this flattering, like they were sort of begging me to stay, even though I knew it wasn't my dazzling personality and intellect they'd be missing, but my money. I had to choose a major if I stayed, and I was still a little bit into everything—and, to tell you the truth, I knew I wasn't really genius at anything yet—so choosing one now seemed like a risky idea. People make it out like becoming an adult, with a real job and all that, is this big hard thing to accomplish, but to me it doesn't seem that way. I mean, when I'm ready to be some hot shit accountant or whatever, believe me, I'll go back and get the degree, and before anyone knows what happened I'll be picking up the check all the time.

Besides, I was waiting tables full time at this tourist trap, bringing scared-looking people ten-dollar slices of New York cheesecake made in some Milwaukee factory. And the manager may have been this jackass pedophile that I often imagined murdering in the most dramatic scenarios, but I still liked waiting tables a whole lot better than going to class. The money was great, and, at least in my experience, it's the people who never finished college who are the smartest. Or at least the nicest, which is just as well. People with degrees tend to spend most of their time making sure everyone around them feels real dumb.

Mom wasn't so into my dropping out. As close as I am to her, there's still some things that I'll just do, like out of nowhere, and leaving school was one of them. All the paperwork was done before Mom even knew. We had a pretty tense chat about it, but then Mom just got all quiet on the line. I asked her what's wrong and she said nothing, nothing at all.

Then you know what she says?

"Hey, it's your life now."

"Wait. What do you mean exactly?"

"Just what I said."

Is it me, or are mothers always saying things like this, these subtle things that remind you of how much of an idiot you can be? I don't know. Truth is, I'll probably go back pretty soon. You've got to understand, this was only a few months ago, and I've basically just been hanging around since. I'm just kind of tired, real tired actually, and trying to relax. I just wanted to make some money, still do. I'll tell you, there may be some good colleges here, but

New York is a horrible place to go to school. Unless you're rich. If you have money, you might be okay. You might be able to feel productive. But it just drove me mad. Everyone around you is working, making money, and all the while you're stuck staring out the window of some classroom, getting poorer and poorer, going into tremendous debt. It makes it impossible to concentrate on what the teacher's telling you about some ancient theory, some stone tablature. Like is it really worth tens of thousands to know what the Rosetta Stone is, when if you're really dying to know you can just buy a book about it for a couple bucks?

———

"You know somethin'?" Dad was saying. "I've never lived alone."

I thought this was a peculiar thing to say. I had actually thought about this before, when I first moved into my apartment, that he'd never lived on his own. A lot of getting older has been figuring out these kinds of things about Dad. I decided to ignore him.

"Are you getting hungry?" I asked.

"You know me," he said. "I can always eat."

There was something about the way he said this. I don't know. It's such a simple, meaningless thing, that probably everyone says a thousand times before he dies. But right now Dad's tone made it sound important, and not just because he barely ate anything when I knew him. He just sounded really out of it.

"Are you okay?" I asked. "You sound a little, I don't know, tired."

"Oh, I'm fine, feller," he said. "You're right. I'm just tired. Tired as hell."

"What are you in the mood for, for food?"

"Oh, anything you want, feller," Dad said. "You know me."

"Well," I said.

I pretended to mull this over for a second, like I was thinking of every single restaurant in the city. That way Dad wouldn't detect that I already had it all planned out. It was a covert operation.

"I know this seafood place," I said. "It's supposed to be great."

———

Dad just ordered a martini, a beer for me.

It was around one in the afternoon, an hour I typically don't spend drinking beer but I figured I'd make an exception for Dad. The restaurant was actually pretty fantastic, lots of marble, these high ceilings laden with plastic leaves and flowers—it was in an old bank, so that's why it was so ornate. It's kind of funny to think that a bank can go out of business these days and make more money as a restaurant, but what do I know?

I just liked looking around the place. You should have seen the hostesses—you'd have given up a thumb to suck one of their toes. And everyone was so clean-looking. You know the type, like they'd sacrificed the chance at ever having interesting thoughts in their heads for eternal youth. Half of them were wired with one of those cellular phones that you jam right up in your ear. You know, so it was impossible to determine if they were talking to the person next to them, or someone on the phone, or if they were just babbling to themselves like a homeless person.

I'll be honest. I can fit in pretty well with these types. Even though I'm from Rockville I was pretty much meant to be from New York. I don't carry a cellular phone or anything, don't kid myself that I can afford one, but I still find myself on dates with some of these real clean women. My two years in New York, I've gotten in the habit of going out with a lot of older women, like thirty-year-olds, even ones older than that. I told you, people are always thinking I'm a lot older than I am.

I'm just always convinced older women will understand everything, but every time they end up just as misguided as the girls my age—just as misguided as *me*. Half the time they end up crying to me about something like their jobs. They want me to give them all the answers, I swear. And all

I ever want is for them to stop touching my face like that. I'm trying to get better about all this, I just don't really know how.

I guess I'm just saying that it was nice having Dad here with me, in the restaurant. That's all. Screwed up as he was, the guy was the only honest-looking person in the place. I almost felt bad about the dent it was about to make in his finances.

"Didja get a look at that hostess?"

"Oh yeah" I said. "The women in New York are ridiculous."

"They're all bitches?"

"Yeah," I said. "Pretty much. How's your drink?"

"Damn good," he said. "Wanna taste?"

"I'm cool," I said. "Hey, wanna know something funny?"

I had so many stories I was dying to tell Dad, and this one was probably top of the list.

"What's up?"

"You know I wait tables, right?" I began.

"No," he said. "You do? You work in restaurants?"

"Yeah," I said. "Anyway, I was subbing for the bartender the other day and this woman comes in at like three in the afternoon and orders a martini. I make it with vodka and vermouth, and she flips! Gives me this whole lecture on how it's a gin drink. She goes on and on. It's gin, it's gin.

She was around ninety, but I still didn't believe her. So I look it up, and it turns out she's right," I said. "And you know what? It's your damn fault I was wrong."

"Well," Dad said, "cheers to that!"

I couldn't tell if he actually understood what I was talking about. But just then he seemed happy, like himself, tapping his glass to mine, the icy liquid all coming right up to the lip but not spilling over—so I didn't care. I'm telling you, the guy was in bad shape. I don't know if I've been clear enough on this. Like on the phone, he really sounded depressed. And seeing him in person, he had this kind of deflated walk. It had nothing to do with the paunch. And I don't just mean he seemed worn out from having to deal with the painful life he had up in Jersey, drilled into a hunchback by Mary and her yelling, Melanie and her wet little face and noisy eyes, by this new kid, little Raymond, my Asian clone. You could just tell there was probably more, something else.

Which is why I was like—

"So Dad, what's going on?"

"I don't know, feller," he said. He took a sip of his drink. "I guess you could call it marital issues."

"Oh God, that's *right*!" I said. "You're *married* now! I completely forgot!"

It's a bizarre thing, when you realize you can't even remember if your father is married or not.

"I am," Dad said. "I sure am."

"And how's the kid?" I said. "How old is he now?"

"Two," Dad said. "Ray is two years old, and he really is great. You gotta see him sometime. He really is a lot like you."

A year or so ago this would have killed me. I would have ended up smiling, excusing myself, then finding something sharp to dig into the back of my hand. But I'm trying not to get all hung up on things like this anymore. I mean, overall I think being angry is a good thing—it tends to mean you probably just love everything around you a little too much. But it's not worth getting angry about things that have nothing to do with you, things that don't matter, like your father's kid, and him comparing it to you all the time. Trust me. It's just not good for you.

"Well, that's good," is all I said. "And Melanie? How's she doing?"

"You know," he said. "She's a handful. She's turning into a beautiful girl though."

"Really?" I said.

"No joke," Dad said.

"She was a tough one," I said. I used to hate that girl, as you know. Now I just don't care about her at all. "So what's up with Mary?" I asked.

Right then his face gets all still, like very serious. It was funny. You could tell he wanted to say something, but before he could open his mouth the waitress came by. She was nice-looking, wavy brown hair, and the kind of freckles on her face that just made you want to take her to the beach, somewhere sunny. You know, just so you could watch them multiply.

Dad's like me in the sense that he immediately cheers up in the presence of a nice-looking waitress. He was all perked up now, his face lit up, really alive. I didn't blame him. The women in the town he lived in in Jersey were all pretty much cyclopes.

So he went wild with the ordering. I didn't even have to slyly egg him on, to get him to spend a thousand dollars. My plan was brilliantly passive-aggressive. Dad was ordering oysters and lobster tails and scallops in some hundred dollar sauce. He ordered eggs with crabmeat. He ordered every side dish. He even asked to hold on to a menu, in case there was something he'd missed. The waitress seemed genuinely amused. Dad's good that way. With women he doesn't know, he can make them feel incredible. It's a talent. I can do the exact same thing.

"And I suppose we need another round," he added.

————

"Hey, you know who I saw not too long ago?" I asked as the next round was delivered.

"Who's that?"

"Shirley," I said.

"Well, I'll be damned," he said. "She still look incredible?"

"She does."

She'd called up Mom during my last year of high school because she was in A.A. and one of the steps is to call up all the people you screwed over and take them out to dinner or whatever. She was something like forty, but looked fantastic, she really did. She was going to college, was bartending at some fancy hotel bar in D.C. It's funny how hardcore drunks always end up as bartenders. We ate, the three of us, at a Mexican restaurant, some chain on Rockville Pike, and Shirley ordered Mom's margarita, with some fancy tequila, and smelled it to make sure the proportions were right. I knew about the cocaine and everything at this point, and I remember being amazed that her nose still worked so well.

"Shirley," Dad sighed. "I can't believe it."

I guess I was curious about Dad and Shirley, and about Dad and cocaine, because I never really knew what the deal was and at least would like to be able to tell you something about it. I guess that's why I brought her up with him. But suddenly I wanted to change the subject. That's the problem with me. I never know what I really want until just after it's happened. So I'm sorry.

———

"So," I said, "can you believe I actually live here? In New York?"

"I'll be damned," he said. "How's school?"

"It's all right."

"It's important," Dad said, all serious in a way that made you want to laugh. People who didn't get degrees when they were young are always telling you how important they are, like their lives would have been so different if they'd known that at the time. But if you grew up around people like Dad, you know these types don't really have any idea what they're talking about.

That's why I didn't bother telling him I had dropped out, but just changed the subject again. I brought up women again, New York women in particular, because you could always sidetrack Dad by bringing up women. He probably commented on every one that walked by, about their height, their walks, how their skin looked so tight they probably couldn't even blink right. I don't know why, but I found myself telling him that I go out with women like that all the time. It's not true. I guess I wanted to make him jealous.

But now, as the oysters came, and as we started in on our third round, I was getting antsy to bring up Mary again. For some reason I was very curious about Dad's marital issues, even though I'd barely known he was married.

"So what's up with Mary?" I said.

"It's a tough thing," Dad said. "It's really a tough thing."

Just then I knew exactly what was going on. You could tell by how vague Dad was being. People are always vague like that when they're the ones at fault. But that's not saying they still don't want you to pry it out of them.

So I asked—

"Is it what I think it is?"

"That depends," Dad said.

"What's her name?" I said.

Dad picked up his martini, and in one sip he finished it off, old school, just sort of funneled it coolly down his throat, waiting until it was in his stomach to swallow. His eyes got glossy now. Dad's eyes can get like that in a second, glossy and dry-looking at the exact same time. It's disturbing to witness. He wiped his upper lip. There used to be a moustache there, when I knew him. I couldn't get over that.

"Why are you so smart?" he was now saying. He sounded all relieved, practically excited. "When did you get so damn smart?"

"I knew it!" I said. I was excited myself. "I thought so on the phone. I could just tell."

The waitress must have had some fine-tuned radar that alerted her when someone's drink was empty. Because Dad had just finished the martini, and here she was, coming over like she was on wheels, asking about another round. I'm a waiter too, and a pretty good one. I don't work at that tourist trap anymore, but a much more classy place. Still, I always forget to ask people about their drinks. It just slips my mind. They always end up having to ask me.

"When did he get so smart?" Dad was asking the waitress. "Can you help me figure out when my son got so smart?"

"I have no idea," she said. She looked pretty much my age, but you could tell she had a different background and just didn't get it. My problem is I can tell this right away, with pretty much everyone I meet.

"This is my son," Dad was saying. "This is my son."

I just looked at the waitress and smiled. Like don't worry, everything's okay. She didn't seem to know how to talk to Dad anymore.

"The oysters, by the way, are terrific," Dad was saying.

"Thank you," she said. I think she was still looking at me though. "I'll be right back with another round."

"I could marry that woman," Dad said.

"I heard you were already married," I said. I was eager to return to the subject at hand. "She's younger, isn't she?" I asked.

Dad sipped his martini. It didn't seem to bother him that there was nothing left. He was also nodding. He was saying yes. Yes, she was younger—

"Like thirty-five?" I said. Dad was forty-three now.

"Oh, a little younger," he said. The martini glass was still right up against his lip.

"Thirty?"

"Younger."

"Jesus, Dad!"

"I know it, feller."

"Well how old is she?"

It was making me kind of sick to keep on guessing. If she turned out to be fourteen, I'd rather hear it from Dad than from my own mouth.

"She's young," Dad said. "She's great, though. She really is."

"How old is she?"

Dad looks at me here and smiles. Actually, he was looking past me, but my head was in the way. On his mouth was the kind of smile certain people get—charismatic types, mainly—when they're nervous, when they just want someone to smile back but know their odds are pretty slim. For a second I thought he was about to start laughing.

But then he was talking again.

"Twenty," he was now saying. "She's twenty years old."

I didn't really lose it. That's the strange thing. You can find out your father is going out with a girl exactly your age and you'd be surprised how little affect it has on you, especially if you don't really know your father anymore. I just sort of nodded at him, said Jesus Christ a few times, and waited for my drink to arrive. I don't think I was smiling. I ate a piece of bread. I looked around at all the people in the restaurant. Look at them: they really are all so clean-looking.

————

The food at this place really was spectacular, I have to say. Dad, in his zealous state, had ordered so much that our entire table was cluttered with a million different entreés and side dishes. Dad used to work in restaurants, so it was nice to see that he was pleased with the food.

God, it really was incredible. He was telling me all about this little twenty-year-old girl of his. Her name was Jenny. He had gone to school to become a vascular technician, but he'd met Jenny at his job before that, the one at the Ding Dong Deli. She worked there too, had the shift before his, but sometimes she'd stick around.

Telling me all this, Dad was getting all relaxed and excited, disturbingly so. Dad was telling me that because he had the graveyard shift the place was often empty for hours. And since Dad never knows when to shut up, he went on to add that sometimes he'd lock the door and they'd have sex all over the deli. He kept referring to Jenny as very athletic. He couldn't get over how fit this young girl was, and me, I just couldn't get over any of it. I mean, what do you do when a guy like this happens to be your father? Where do you go from there?

"So Mary's goin' crazy," he suddenly said.

"What do you mean?"

"Well, you know how she was always a little insane?" he asked.

Can you believe he actually just said this?

"Of course," is all I said.

"Well, she started suspecting something," Dad said, "and she started examining the phone bills."

"Jesus," I said. "That's ridiculous."

"I know," he said. "So she suspects something, because there were all these calls to Jenny. But I'll tell you, it's really special with her. It really is."

I believed him. The whole thing sounds so absurd, I see that now, and it wasn't that long ago that I saw him, a few months really. There's Dad, telling me about some girl who happens to be my age, telling me what it's like to get with her in the yogurt aisle of all places, and still, it seemed normal enough.

Dad was still going, talking about Jenny—

"I mean, I've tried to end it plenty of times, especially once Mary started flippin' out, but I just can't."

"Dad," I said. "Your life is such a mess."

"I know," he said. "It's pretty funny, huh?"

"It's hysterical," I said. "Why don't you just get a divorce?"

"How's your mother?" he asked.

"She's great," I said. I didn't want to talk about Mom,

though. At this point, Mom has nothing to do with him. "Seriously Dad, you should get a divorce."

"Where's that waitress?" Dad asked. "You see our waitress?"

———

Look at him! Just look at him!

Dad's cracking up now. His face all red, eyes the same color. He's laughing so hard he's not making any sounds, looks like he's sweating. He's slapping the table. I guess I look the same way, because I'm laughing too, just as hard, pounding the table too.

"They all shave!" he was saying.

"They sure do!" I said.

"*All* of them?"

"Pretty much!"

We'd finished our food at this point, had ordered a few more rounds of drinks. I lost track of how many, probably something like seven each at this point. I'm not such a big drinker, so I was pretty out of it. Dad didn't seem to be in much better shape. I'll be twenty-one soon, and sometimes I worry I'll be sick of drinking completely by the time I can do it legally.

"I can't believe it!" he was saying. "It's really fantastic!"

"I know it!"

He really couldn't get over it. We'd abandoned talking seriously about his marriage dilemma. I had told him a few more times that he should just get a divorce, but he didn't really want to hear it. That was it. I mean, what more could I have said? What better advice could I have offered the guy?

So now we were just talking about women. I wish you'd have been there. I've never had a brother, but right now that's exactly how Dad came off, like my older brother. We were talking in such explicit detail, the kind of talk that drives girls mad. Dad just couldn't get over how they shaved themselves, girls my age, how the clipped their pubic hair to Astroturf. It was one of Jenny's greatest attributes.

"It's so much better," he was now saying. He wasn't laughing so hard anymore. But he seemed happy as hell. I couldn't tell how I felt exactly.

"I guess it is," I said.

"Women my age," Dad said, "it's like a jungle down there! You need a machete and a flashlight!"

What's so funny about Dad's saying this is that I knew exactly what he was talking about. Have I been clear enough on this? About me and older women? I don't know what it is. I just find it easier to get them to go out with me than girls my own age. I suppose you might say I have some sort of fetish, if you were a psychoanalyst or someone with that kind of mind. Me, I just try not to think about it.

But I knew about their bodies. I knew how they were so

much less timid when it came to taking off their clothes, how it sometimes freaked you out how they were suddenly standing there naked. I know how certain parts of them are more developed, more sensitive, how you can get them to whimper sometimes just by placing your tongue on the back of their knees. And I know about the skin on their hands, how maybe it is more wrinkled, okay, but it's also softer, and I know how they're more precise with how they touch you, more caring, even though you barely ever get aroused and end up thinking about Claudia of all people. I know how with older women you end up sticking your face so deep in their hair, just because you hope it'll get dark enough that you'll end up seeing Liz maybe. What's wrong with you? I know how all you ever want with them is to apologize. You don't even know why, but you always want to apologize, to everyone really. I know that. You'd say I'm sorry before you said hello, nice to meet you. I know this. Is it okay? Is it fine? Am I fine? Am I okay? I don't know. I don't know. You just want to say I'm sorry, you just don't want to disappoint. I don't want to disappoint anyone. I don't want to disappoint you. I'm sorry. I know it's not my fault but still. I'm sorry. I'm so sorry—

"Hey, you okay?" Dad was saying all of a sudden.

"What?"

"Everything fine? You look like you might be—"

"What do you mean? I think so."

"Just checkin'."

"Oh, yeah. I'm just a little tired lately."

"I hear that."

"Real tired," I said.

—so of course I knew what Dad was talking about, that's all I was saying. I knew what it was like when women his age slid their underwear down. Except that I kind of prefer it this way. I don't know. I just like how it's so much less obvious.

But I wasn't about to bring any of that up with Dad. You tell me: what would be the point?

———

The waitress was coming by again, and Dad was asking her again when did I get so smart. He told her again that I was his son. He couldn't get enough of this.

"This is my son," he was saying. "Isn't that funny?"

"Everything's okay over here?" she said.

"Look at him!" Dad said. "That's my son!"

"Can I take away some of these plates?"

"Sure," I said.

"I have two sons," Dad said.

"Hey, there, Dad," I said.

"I have two sons—"

"Dad."

"—and they don't know each other," he said. "They've never met."

She looked about as uncomfortable as people get, but I didn't care about her anymore. I was just looking at Dad, wanted to see how long he'd go on. She'd bring us more drinks no matter what, and right now that's all that mattered.

And we just laughed, kept on laughing, more and more, until the whole place was pretty much empty and our laughter was practically shattering the windows. We talked about sleeping with twenty-year-old girls until there was absolutely nothing left to say. We didn't talk about anything real again, but I wasn't too worried about Dad's future. You knew what it would be like for him, so there was no point feeling that bad. Feeling bad for people like Dad just ends up making you feel like an idiot. That's really all it is with him. I mean, for the most part, there's just no point.

———

The bill came now. The waitress was all quick to drop it off and get back to doing something else. I didn't blame her. It must have come to hundreds of dollars, but throwing down all those twenties, Dad didn't even flinch. Talk about anti-climactic, right? He just paid and asked am I ready to get going. I guess he had the money, or at least Mary did. I was fine with this.

"Wait a second?" I asked once we were outside. "Did you quit smoking?"

"I quit years ago."

"You did?"

"Right around the time I lost the moustache."

"Oh," I said. It hit me then that there were a lot of things like this, small bits of information I didn't know. Insignificant maybe, but I wanted to know them anyway. But I knew it would take a while.

So we walked to his car now, stumbled is more like it, and said good-bye. He said we should stay in better touch, or maybe I said it. It didn't matter. He had a minivan of all things, a used one that he'd fixed up. I wasn't too concerned about Dad's driving home. He was drunk as hell, I know, but I wasn't worried still. And not just because I figured he'd been driving drunk for years, was probably a genius at it. It's that Dad just isn't the type of person who ends up having one too many, getting in a car, and swerving into the median and dying. Dad's not the type to put himself through the windshield. It's simple. I know I'm the same way, maybe even more so. Some people can get away with pretty much anything, and not end up through a windshield. It's hard to explain. I mean, I guess you could call this good luck. But only if you really wanted to.

ACKNOWLEDGMENTS

Where to start, where to start—

Thank you to all friends and family—literally and figuratively, nothing would be possible without you. Specifically, thank you: Christiana Sadigianis, who sat through my reading aloud (in a state of near nervous breakdown) each chapter of this book as I wrote it, allowing me to use the expressions on her wonderful face as a sort of boredom barometer; Rachel "Ether" Hartford, who read and edited early versions like a star; Mike Johns, fearless eater of deep-fried crab claws; Sarah Wells and Jess Perlmeter, for being so insanely smart and stunning all these years; Joanna Coles, who claims she's a cynical woman, but doesn't know what she's talking about because her optimism and enthusiasm have been inspiring from the second I met her (even if her British accent makes me feel hopelessly unsophisticated); Omi, for being the hippest grandmother a grandson could ask for; Kim Peirce, for always helping me separate the bullshit that matters from the bullshit that doesn't; Sara Stewart, the number one female bodysurfer on the East Coast, who . . . well, what can I really say here, Sara?

Thank you, Jennifer Hershey, for the obvious.

Many thanks to Sarah Durand and everyone at William Morrow/HarperCollins, and to my agent, Melanie Jackson, a woman so flat-out magnificent that I'm still convinced I've made her up.

Mom . . . you know anything I try to say will only be an understatement. But here goes, old school: I thank you infinity times infinity, and love you infinity times more.

And thank you, Dad, specifically for the dirt-bike rides and the leather jacket and for introducing me to raw oysters at age two. They're still my favorite food.